"Bella." Her name emerged sounding far too deep, and not at all casual and disinterested. Luc cleared his throat and spoke again. "Come inside."

Bella looked into Luchino's dark, beautiful eyes and warned herself not to show any sign of awareness. But his gentleness toward his daughter undermined the clear-cut nature of Bella's opinions of him, and that left her vulnerable.

She mustn't forget all he had done. If she did, she might fall prey to the way he made her feel. She might even fall for him again.

"Good evening, Luc." Bella stepped forward. She had some vain hope of passing him, of moving into the house and keeping a sensible half a room of distance between them from that point on.

Luc didn't let her pass.

"Arabella, you look ravishing." He wrapped his hand around her upper arm  it was so Mediterrane and nice, that she sim grip her arms and sm leaned in to place a sw

Dear Reader,

Few things can give us a greater sense of worth and security than being part of a loving family, whose members are ready to prop us up when we're scared or pressured, to celebrate our successes and to share our heartaches.

Sometimes that family comprises a traditional core of loving parents and cherished children. At other times our "families" are a more eclectic mix. When we first meet the Gable sisters in Chrissy's story, *Her Millionaire Boss,* we discover the joy and support to be found among sisters who are making it in life without the benefit of loving elders.

In many ways, Bella, the heroine of *The Italian Single Dad,* has been that loving elder, the one who carried much of the responsibility, the worry and the determination to see her sisters thrive. Now it's Bella's turn to find a different kind of love in the unexpected guise of single dad Luchino Montichelli and his beautiful daughter, Grace.

Will they overcome the hurt that tore Luc's life apart, and the history that makes Bella question her ability to let others in?

I hope you enjoy finding out in Luc and Bella's story.

Hugs,

Jennie

JENNIE ADAMS
The Italian Single Dad

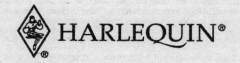

HARLEQUIN®

TORONTO • NEW YORK • LONDON
AMSTERDAM • PARIS • SYDNEY • HAMBURG
STOCKHOLM • ATHENS • TOKYO • MILAN • MADRID
PRAGUE • WARSAW • BUDAPEST • AUCKLAND

If you purchased this book without a cover you should be aware that this book is stolen property. It was reported as "unsold and destroyed" to the publisher, and neither the author nor the publisher has received any payment for this "stripped book."

ISBN-13: 978-0-373-03977-7
ISBN-10:   0-373-03977-8

THE ITALIAN SINGLE DAD

First North American Publication 2007.

Copyright © 2007 by Jennifer Ann Ryan.

All rights reserved. Except for use in any review, the reproduction or utilization of this work in whole or in part in any form by any electronic, mechanical or other means, now known or hereafter invented, including xerography, photocopying and recording, or in any information storage or retrieval system, is forbidden without the written permission of the publisher, Harlequin Enterprises Limited, 225 Duncan Mill Road, Don Mills, Ontario, Canada M3B 3K9.

This is a work of fiction. Names, characters, places and incidents are either the product of the author's imagination or are used fictitiously, and any resemblance to actual persons, living or dead, business establishments, events or locales is entirely coincidental.

This edition published by arrangement with Harlequin Books S.A.

® and TM are trademarks of the publisher. Trademarks indicated with ® are registered in the United States Patent and Trademark Office, the Canadian Trade Marks Office and in other countries.

www.eHarlequin.com

Printed in U.S.A.

Australian author **Jennie Adams** grew up in a rambling farmhouse surrounded by books, and by people who loved reading them. She decided at a young age to be a writer, but it took many years and a lot of scenic detours before she sat down to pen her first romance novel. Jennie is married with two adult children, and has worked in a number of careers and voluntary positions, including transcription typist and preschool assistant. Jennie makes her home in a small inland city in New South Wales. In her leisure time she loves taking long, rambling walks, starting knitting projects that she rarely finishes, chatting with friends, trips to the movies and new dining experiences.

Jennie loves to hear from her readers, and can be contacted via her Web site at www.jennieadams.net.

For my friends Jennifer and Lynell.
Thank you for your support.
And with thanks to Susan, Pazit, and Lina.

PROLOGUE

TWENTY-YEAR-OLD Arabella Gable took her seat behind two of the other models, and waited for the plane to take off. As Italy grew smaller beneath them, she finally let out a breath.

Her second trip to the country was over, the payment for the fashion shoot safe in her bank account where she and her sisters could benefit from it. From now on she would work only within Australia. She certainly had no desire to come back to Italy again. The country was beautiful, but the reminders of Luchino, of the mistake she had made, of how he'd preyed on her and hidden things from her, were too strong, even after almost a year.

A stewardess offered in-flight headphones to those who wanted to listen to music. Bella took a pair and nodded her thanks.

'I can't believe you saw him, Karen.' In the seat in front of her, one of the models spoke. 'I'm so jealous. Apparently he travels all over Europe now. What are the odds of you stumbling across him in Naples?' The older model, Lareen, had a deep, carrying voice.

Bella wasn't interested. She stared out of the window and wished herself home with her sisters in their cosy flat in Melbourne. Were they both OK? Had the money and provisions really lasted, or had they said so when she phoned simply so she wouldn't worry?

'Yes, I saw "Mr Diamonds" himself! Not the older brother. Who'd want him? But *Luc* Montichelli… Oh, yes.' Karen giggled. 'He could show me his assets any time.'

'Mr Diamonds'? Luc Montichelli?

Bella's breath stopped in her throat. Her worry over her sisters suspended for a moment. Luchino had been in Naples? Right there where she might have bumped into him?

She had felt safe from the chance of seeing him. Had believed he would be in Milan, where he made his home, otherwise she wouldn't have come, would have found some other way to tide the finances over until her new contract started next month. Bella's heart raced and a fresh well of hurt and betrayal rose up. She hated that just the mention of his name could do that to her.

I'm over him. It doesn't hurt any more. It doesn't!

Oh, but dear lord. She could have stumbled right into Luchino and his *wife and child*. What if they'd been travelling together, on holiday, or lived in Naples now or something?

Thank God she *hadn't* seen them. The models continued to talk about Luchino, his looks, how much money he had. Bella didn't want to know what Luchino did, or where he was, or how he looked or sounded or anything else.

Luchino was a blot on her life, a horrible, hurtful error she never wanted to repeat. She would never be gullible like that with a man again. Bella fumbled to pull the earphones from their packaging so she could drown the voices out. The plastic covering crackled between her fingers, but refused to open.

Lareen spoke again. 'I don't know if I'd want to tangle with him, though.'

'Why not?' Karen responded with curiosity to the hint of warning in the other model's tone.

'Because I think he might be too ruthless to handle, honey.' Lareen went on. 'I heard he divorced his wife and got custody of his kid, then stuck the kid away in a house in a remote village with only a nanny to watch over her and simply never goes near them. You have to admit, that's cold-blooded.'

'Really?' Karen gasped. 'When did the divorce happen?'

'I'm not sure, but they've been apart at least a few months.' Lareen paused for a moment. 'He doesn't look like the same person now. That's what struck me when I saw him. He's got this anger in his eyes…'

Bella sat completely still. Her heart raced. She could barely believe what she'd heard. It shocked her enough that Luc's marriage had ended, although maybe she should have expected it. After all, he hadn't exactly been faithful. But to snatch his child from her mother's arms, and then abandon that child was unforgivable. *That* wrenched at Bella's heart, because she knew just how much it hurt.

Unaware of Bella's shock behind her, Lareen went on. 'He must have taken the baby just to punish his wife or something. Divorces can be ugly.'

'Are you sure this is true, Lareen?' Karen sounded uncertain, but hungry for more information.

Bella clenched her hands in her lap as she wrestled with her feelings. She still felt raw inside from her parents' desertion of her and her sisters two years ago. Despite Luchino's deceit last year in Milan when he blatantly pursued her and hid his married state from her, a part of Bella didn't want to believe he would abandon his child.

She didn't want to believe anyone would do that. Some days she still struggled to accept it had happened to her and her sisters. Until she went back to their apartment and looked in the cupboards to check if they had enough food to last them, enough money in the rent jar, and reality smacked her in the face all over again.

Bella tried to protect her sisters from the worst of the worries, but they weren't stupid. They knew, and knowing … hurt them, undermined Bella's efforts to ensure they felt safe and guarded and comfortable.

A wave of protective anger washed through Bella. And that anger, which had focused solely on her parents for two years, now began to turn towards Luchino as well. He had pursued Bella when he had a wife and baby. Bella had fallen most of the way in love, thought it was the real thing. It hurt so much when his wife turned up and Bella realised Luc had simply been toying with her.

Bella learned from that, built walls to protect her heart. But even with all of that, she hadn't imagined Luc could do such a thing as abandon his child.

'It's true.' Lareen's voice deepened even further as she seemed to tap into Bella's very thoughts. 'My cousin, the one who went through Europe on a work visa a while back, got a job in that same village. She went out with the grocery delivery guy, and he told her *everything*.'

Lareen's voice lowered even more. 'The nanny had her friend at the house one day when the guy delivered the groceries. She told her friend Luc just stayed away. He paid the bills, but he wanted nothing to do with the child.'

They went on to talk about how it might feel to be abandoned.

As though they would know anything about it!

Hands shaking, Bella finally got the headphones free of their wrapping, put them over her ears, and plugged into the airline music.

But she didn't hear it. She only heard the rising tide of her disgust and condemnation of a man she had thought she couldn't despise any more.

At least the baby had someone's care. Bella consoled herself with that, but she would never forget what she had learned today.

Not ever.

CHAPTER ONE

HE STALKED into Melbourne's *Maria's* at a minute before closing time on a warm, still summer afternoon, a tall Mediterranean man among the laden shelves of fine Egyptian handbags, Parisian scarves and the feathered and veiled confections that earned the name 'hat' within Australia's haute couture. Racks of designer gowns fluttered in his wake.

'Good afternoon and welcome to *Maria's*. May I help you with anything in particular?' The words fell from Arabella Gable's lips, polite, professional. She guarded herself too well to allow any hint of impatience or weariness at the end of a busy day to colour her words.

The man turned his head and Bella suppressed a gasp as a flood of memories stripped time away. Six years ago *this man had held her heart in his hands.*

Bella's throat tightened as feelings rushed through her. Fury, hurt, disillusionment. Yet as she looked at him, the barriers around her heart shook. It must be from her anger.

And from shock. You didn't expect to ever see him again.

Why was he here? Her mind sought answers, but didn't find them.

'When I explain matters, you'll have little choice but to

help me.' The rich, smooth accent of his Italian heritage shivered over her, so familiar, once so dear.

Never again.

'Luchino.' His name emerged on a whisper of sound. She had believed him out of her life forever. What brought him to Australia, to Melbourne? Here, to *Maria's*? Against her will, Bella's gaze roved across his features, took them in as she had in Milan all those years ago. Dark hair, dark brows, angular chin, chocolate-brown eyes and a mouth made for seduction, all of it packaged in the sculpted aplomb of Armani, pure black.

From the fitted shirt to the dress trousers and leather belt that encased slim hips and long legs, Luchino Montichelli shouted wealth, power and sensuality.

Banked anger lurked in the backs of his eyes.

'Yes, it's Luc—one and the same. It's been a long time, Arabella.' His gaze moved over her. Lowered lids hooded his expression, but not before Bella saw the leashed awareness in his eyes. 'The years seem to have favoured you.'

Her heart skipped a beat in reaction to that examination. Not because she reacted in kind! No. But how dared he look at her like that? Her nerves on edge, Bella lifted a slim hand to the knot of blonde hair secured at her nape, then cursed herself for the movement, which might be interpreted as awareness of his interest.

'They've been good to you, too.' She made the grudging admission. 'You look...well.'

Appealing, dangerous, strong and determined and somehow even harder, tougher than the Luc she had known. But then, he'd made some tough moves, hadn't he? Conscienceless ones. Like taking his child from her mother then ignoring her himself. 'Why are you here, Luchino? How could I possibly help you with anything?'

Even the sound of his name on her lips battered at a place deep inside her.

'I never planned to see you again, Arabella.' Luc's mouth tightened as he went on. 'I assure you, I would rather not be here.'

'You'd rather not see me? I'm afraid I return that sentiment.' Bella tossed the words at him, yet for a moment she caught a softer expression in his eyes and her heart—that betraying creature—remembered something that had seemed so special, so right, and a soft vulnerability welled up inside her.

Bella stamped down hard on the reaction. Those memories were an illusion! 'I'm about to close the store so whatever you're here for...'

Maria would kill her for trying to push a customer out of the place. Bella didn't doubt that her boss's Milanese accent would thicken with anger, too. Well, too bad. These were extenuating circumstances, Luchino didn't appear to be here as a customer, and in any case Maria wasn't here to say anything. She was at a fashion expo in Queensland.

'By all means, lock the store.' A well-shaped hand gestured towards the front door. 'Better still, give me the key and I'll do it for you while you put the remainder of the day's takings into the safe. What I have to say to you is best said in private.'

'What would you know about closing procedures?' But his family owned jewellery stores dotted all over Europe and various other parts of the world. Those stores would all follow the same basic closing actions as here.

Luchino had learned his jewellery-design skills in one of the family's stores, or so he had once said. She pushed the thought aside. His career didn't matter to her. *Luchino* no longer mattered to her, except to act as a warning not to allow anyone to hurt her again. 'Anyway, I'm not sure I want to speak with you alone. We didn't exactly part as friends, in case you've forgotten.'

'I've forgotten none of it.' The words sounded like a threat as his gaze moved over her.

What did he see aside from pale, smooth skin, eyes a lighter shade of brown than his, and bone structure that Bella frankly thought too strong and angular to be truly appealing? Why should she care what he thought, anyway?

'And I run a store a mere few city blocks from here.' His gaze drifted away from her, to the racks of clothes, the hats and scarves and handbags. 'I think I can work out how to secure this place.'

'That's you?' Bella tried not to let shock colour her tone of voice. A *Diamonds by Montichelli* store had opened here two weeks ago. Bella had seen it in the papers and dismissed it from her mind. She strove to sound only mildly interested now. 'I thought the new store was an offshoot of the Sydney store, that there'd be a local manager. I thought you focused on design, anyway.'

I thought I would never have to see you again. I don't want to see you!

Each time Bella's sisters had suffered or worried or felt scared over the past five years, a part of Bella had silently linked Luchino to that pain because he was an abandoner, too, just like their parents. And he had hurt Bella, toyed with her emotions when he had no right.

If he intended to remain in Melbourne, if she bumped into him, caught sight of him over and over, how would she cope? The key dropped from her fingers, clattered onto the glass counter, a mockery of the calm control she wanted to portray. 'Have you moved to management? Are you here to get things settled then hand the store over to someone? The Sydney store has a local manager...'

Please let Luchino be about to hand the store over to someone else.

'I no longer work with the family. *Diamonds by Montichelli* is *my* store, a separate entity from all the others. I may share the family name, but ultimately the store will succeed because of *my* work, *my* design and *my* reputation.'

Something painful crossed his face as he spoke the words. He lowered his gaze. His fingers closed around the key. 'I have a lot of roles here—owner, head designer, manager, salesman, craftsman. Whatever is needed at any given time, I do it. I'm here to stay.'

Here to stay and out of sorts with his jewellery-making family? Oh, Bella could relate to that and she didn't want to. She didn't want any common ground with him at all. How could she feel even a mild sympathy for a man who walked away from his child?

'That's why the store isn't called simply *Montichelli's* like the others.'

'That's right.' Luchino turned his broad back to her and strode towards the front of the store. 'Finish up, Arabella, so we can get this discussion over with.'

'I'm leaving in a minute.' Bella made the warning to him, but she had to work to control her shaking hands as she emptied the contents of the cash drawer into a bag and dumped it in the small timed floor safe. Her sheath dress of peach Oriental silk rustled as she moved.

As he turned back towards her, Luchino stopped to examine each of the *Design by Bella* gowns displayed on mannequins to left and right. Despite her anger, Bella's breath hitched as she waited to hear his verdict.

Finally, he spoke. 'You're a woman of hidden talents, Arabella. These are good. At least your skill with design and creation will mean there's half a chance of fixing the mess you've made.'

She had almost relaxed into his praise. Now she pulled herself stiffly upright. 'Mess? What mess?' How dared he say she had made a mess?

'You've gone from modelling, to coercing middle-aged ladies out of huge amounts of money in business ventures that have no guarantee of succeeding.' Accusation tightened every contour of the sculpted face. 'You must really be proud of yourself.'

'Modelling was only ever a job to put money on the table for me and my sis—' She stopped abruptly as she heard herself attempt to justify her earliest choice of career to him.

Then the rest sank in. 'What do you mean? I haven't coerced anybody, and what's it got to do with you, anyway?' Bella *had* hammered out a deal with Maria Rocco, had agreed to bring her designs exclusively to *Maria's* and keep them here on a five-year contract, only if Maria purchased her year's worth of already-created stock up front, but it was a reasonable agreement, because Bella intended to succeed.

'Maria Rocco is my aunt.' As Luchino said it, he watched her face for her reaction. 'That makes this very much my business.'

Bella pulled her face into a tight mask to cover her shock and uncertainty. Maria was Milanese, it was true, but the older woman had lived in Australia almost all her adult life. 'Maria is a Rocco, not a Montichelli, and she told me she has no family.'

Bella clung to that knowledge, even as she noted that Luchino did indeed share some similarities of feature with Maria. That had to be just happenstance, though. What was a nose, after all, or the tilt of a chin?

'My aunt left Milan, left the family and changed her name long ago. She no doubt *considered* herself alone.' Harsh anger radiated from him as he went on. 'I'm sure you saw that as an advantage when you set out to rob her of a vast amount of money.'

'I did not! How do you even know about the agreement I have with her?' She stopped, didn't want to reveal anything to him. But he clearly knew something.

Luc's hand rose to touch a spot above his heart—as though to assure himself of the presence of something in his shirt pocket? And yes, a faint square outline showed there—a photo, perhaps.

Before Bella could wonder about it, the mouth that had once offered soft seduction, had once whispered hungry words, love words to her that were oh, so false, tightened again into a strong, determined line.

'I told my new finance manager I wanted to meet Maria. He'd heard Maria took on a protégé. When he mentioned your name, I asked him to get details for me.'

'That's an invasion of Maria's privacy, and of mine!' One that Luchino had apparently taken in his stride.

'It was a timely intervention.' He accompanied the declaration with a squaring of his shoulders. Low warning filled his tone. 'Estranged or not right at this moment, I won't see Maria go under financially because of you.

'You somehow bullied her into buying a year's worth of designer gowns at an astronomical price with no guarantee whatsoever that any of them would sell, and no way for her to get her money back if they don't. On top of that, you talked her into employing you here to make more gowns which also may not sell.'

His face darkened. 'A five-year contract where Maria carries the burden and risk, and you swim along on the high tide of all that money she's handed to you. Don't bother to deny it.'

Bella frowned. She had slaved over that three-page agree-

ment herself. Luchino made it sound one-sided but it wasn't
an unfair arrangement, because Maria knew Bella's only aim
was success for both of them. Bella pushed the inkling of
unease aside. 'It's an agreement, actually, not a contract.' She
hadn't wanted the expense of a lawyer, but Chrissy's past
boss, Henry Montbank, had helped Bella to make sure the
agreement was water-tight.

'It's robbery in the guise of a work arrangement.'

'You'd call me a thief? How—how dare you?' While Bella
simmered in fury, questions vied for space.

Despite Maria's indications to the contrary, she had a
family? That family was the Montichellis?

One fact lodged deep: Luchino had investigated not only
Maria, but also Bella. 'You've pried into my life, behind my
back, as though you had every right to do that. Just what did
you find out about me, about my sisters? How far did you dig
around, expose us—?'

'I investigated your finances, Arabella, the work you've done
in the years since I last saw you. And I learned everything there
is to know about your arrangement with my aunt. I won't apolo-
gise for doing that.' He said the last with a hard glare in his eyes.

'I intend to reclaim Maria as my aunt.' His expression
softened a little as he said this. 'She's family and...I want that
bond with her if it's at all possible. I'd have arranged to meet
her before now if she hadn't been out of the city.'

A hunger for family was bizarre, given his history. Yet he
seemed sincere. Bella needed to remember he could be both
convincing and duplicitous!

Bella glared right back at him, but sudden weariness
tugged at her. Her hands ached from the hours spent in the
adjoining sewing and consultation room, meticulously stitch-
ing Chinese *cloisonné* beads to the fitted sleeves of her latest
creation while Maria's sales clerk took care of customers.

Bella wanted to go home, slip into one of her black catsuits and indulge in an hour of Pilates in front of the TV.

Instead she had to deal with an angry man she had hoped never to see again, a man who believed she meant his aunt financial harm. 'Despite what you say, you mustn't have investigated very well, Luchino, because Maria is in no financial danger from me.'

'On the contrary, the purchase of your stock almost bankrupted her.' Luchino raked a hand through his thick, dark hair.

Glossy, silky hair with a tendency to wave...

Bella pulled herself up straighter and gave Luc the benefit of her coldest stare. It *was* a lot of money, but she had needed a strong capital injection to enable her to buy the best fabrics and accoutrements to create more gowns, and her designs justified the cost.

It might take a few years, but Maria would get back her investment, and much more, eventually. 'Your aunt is very wealthy, Luchino. She owns a penthouse apartment in the best part of the city, drives the latest-model luxury car and goes on overseas buying trips every other week.

'Maria didn't hesitate to agree to my terms, and she can afford to carry things along until my gowns start to really pay for her.' Bella's employer walked and talked affluence and until this moment Bella had seen no reason to doubt her.

Luchino shook his head. 'Maria has spent beyond her means for years. The apartment is rented, the car is a lease and those buying trips have put her heavily into debt.' His gaze darkened as he looked around the store. 'She was in no position to buy into a speculative venture like yours.'

'My gowns will sell. Maria has made a good investment, and I intend to prove that.' Yet even as Bella said it, her stomach knotted.

She hadn't asked Maria's financial status. She had assumed

it on the evidence in front of her. Now doubt formed and Bella experienced that hated feeling of losing control. If Maria really had no money, just a pile of debts…

'I can't fail.' The words were a stark statement, because she simply couldn't. Failure had ceased to be an option when their parents unforgivably abandoned her, Chrissy and Sophia while her sisters were still in high school. Every struggle since then had underscored that abandonment, and underscored Bella's condemnation of the man before her because he had mirrored her parents' actions.

Bella had striven to succeed, and she had done it. For her sisters, and to assure herself they would all be OK, and now she had to do it to assure herself *she* was OK. 'As I build a client base, more gowns will sell until eventually Maria ends up making a strong profit from her investment.'

But none of that would work if Maria went bankrupt in the meantime.

As the weight of concern pressed down on her, Bella wanted nothing more than to assure herself she could indeed go forward, successfully, as she intended. 'I'll ring Maria. Find out where things really stand.'

Maria could allay Bella's fears, Bella could send Luchino away. All would be well again, except for Luchino's determination to be part of Maria's life, which would bring him into contact with Bella's life.

'I can't allow you to phone my aunt. I don't want her to know that I bought—that I *investigated* her.' He paused and cleared his throat, then said in a grudging tone, 'I want a chance to get to know her without business matters getting in the way.'

Again that reference to a hunger for family. It confused Bella, and all of a sudden she wanted the comfort of *her* family, of hearing her sisters' voices. Her hand reached for her bag beneath the counter, for the cellphone within. She could get either of them with a single press of a button. Then she stopped herself.

Later she could talk to Chrissy and Soph. Right now, if she tried to talk to either of them, she would say too much. Give too much away.

They knew about that ill-fated trip to Milan, but Bella had downplayed its impact on her, left out several vital bits, had not revealed the near-devastation of that whirlwind week when she offered her heart and Luchino seemed about to take it before she discovered the truth about him. She'd been nineteen and so gullible.

'Prevarication is a waste of time, Arabella. The agreement is stacked in your favour. Maria *is* in financial danger because you pushed for the purchase of your gowns. Whether you knew her financial situation or not, your demands were unacceptable and I intend to see that you make up for your actions. These are the facts. Now, I'll give you two choices to repair the damage.'

The planes of his face sharpened as he stared at her. 'The first choice is you pay back every cent she gave to you, and you walk away.'

He had to be kidding. Bella almost laughed, but the expression on his face stopped her. Utter determination. 'This isn't just about money, Luchino. Maria has agreed to help me launch my label, my name. If I took out a loan to buy the gowns back, I wouldn't be able to afford to re-establish myself elsewhere.'

Bella's feeling of panic deepened. 'I don't have the money any more. I invested it in fabrics and notions for new gowns.'

'Then I guess that leaves choice number two.' He took a step towards her and she backed just slightly until she could sense the presence of the service counter behind her.

'Oh? And what is that?' Bella tried not to think about his closeness, tried not to feel threatened and confused by him.

Luchino fired his answer at her. 'It's quite simple, Arabella. You see to it that every gown my aunt bought from you sells quickly and for a good price.'

'Sure. I'll just make that happen.' She would look up a fairy godmother in the yellow pages and get her to wave her magic wand. 'Speed isn't the key ingredient in my work plan. Maria knew that. It's why we agreed on five years.'

What if he's right? What if Maria goes bankrupt?

'Five years is no longer an option. You must go out and attract buyers, attend the best functions, rub shoulders with the most élite of the fashion set, anything it takes to get their interest and sell every last one of those gowns, and sell them fast.'

What did the man want? *I'm just a girl from the suburbs, Luchino. I don't have those kinds of friends.* She lifted her chin to a proud angle. 'Sorry to disappoint you, but I don't have entrée to that crowd.'

'At my side, those doors will open to you.' His grim smile made apprehension claw at her insides. 'You will walk through them, and when you do I will be there. I will stick to you until Maria's financial losses are recouped, one way or another.'

'No.' Close contact with Luchino? Do as he said, dance to his tune? No, no, no! The man must be mad, anyway. Mad about all of it. 'I don't even know if you're telling the truth.'

The locked-up hurt and anger buried in her soul suddenly welled up. 'After all, hiding the truth is what you do, isn't it, Luchino? You pretended you had no wife. Tell me, did it hurt to lose her? Or were you simply glad to be rid of her so you could pursue your affairs conscience-free?'

CHAPTER TWO

'I'M SURPRISED you know about my divorce.' Luc made the observation as his gaze roved Arabella's face. He couldn't seem to take his gaze from her, and the unwelcome resurgence of the old attraction infuriated him.

Bella was as bad as Natalie, out to get what she could by any means available. Bella had proved it in Milan and he almost fell for her act there. She was doing the same thing to Maria now.

Luc would not be taken in a second time. He had no patience for faithless women and their untrustworthy ways.

So why the sudden flare of interest in Arabella after all this time? He had more important things to focus on.

Luc released his hold on Arabella's arm and instead fingered the photo of his daughter that he carried against his heart. Familiar guilt rose up, followed by fierce determination. He would make things right for his daughter somehow. He had to.

'I went to Italy for another modelling shoot five years ago.' She looked as though she wished he would go back to Italy this instant and stay there, too. 'Someone talked about you. I didn't go looking for the information, trust me.'

'Unfortunately, Bella *mia,* I no longer trust anyone, and certainly not you.' In truth the ability to trust had been stripped irrevocably from Luc, stolen away by unexpected betrayal not once, but thrice.

Bella. His brother. His ex-wife. They had all played their part.

Tendrils of ash-blonde hair caressed Bella's neck where they had escaped the knot of hair there. Eyes the colour of rich coffee shone as she seemed to gather herself.

Her anger arced, like light refracted from the planes of a sharp-cut diamond. He shouldn't care, shouldn't picture her with his own Montichelli jewellery designs gracing the long, slender neck. It was the appeal of her physical looks, nothing more. His mouth tightened.

Was it worth it, Arabella? What did the show manager give you in exchange for the use of your body? Money? Help to climb the ladder to greater modelling success?

Perhaps Bella simply felt no remorse. After all, his ex-wife had felt none. In the face of Luc's agonised questions, his brother had shown none.

No more. No thoughts of the past to interfere with the present. No bitterness in this new life.

Australia was a deliberate choice. For...*his daughter.* For Grace. For a fresh start where betrayal could be if not forgotten, at least pushed back into its harsh, dark corner. And Luc had chosen Melbourne because he wanted to get to know the elusive aunt the family had spoken of always in whispers.

'My car is parked a couple of blocks over. The proof of Maria's situation is in it.' Luc snarled the words out as he fought his memories, fought memories of Arabella that still had the ability to move him, even though he knew them to be utterly false. He strode towards the front of the shop. 'Let's go.'

'I'm more than ready to see this so-called proof.' Her hips moved provocatively beneath the silk dress as she collected a matching bag, stalked to the door and flipped the panel of light switches to leave only the night lights burning.

Luc burned, too, in anger, yes, but still with a hint of that old attraction and he didn't want that.

Bella punched a button to arm the alarm system, and waited to hear the series of dull clunks as everything locked behind them. 'The sooner we get to the end of this, the better.'

'I agree.' He took her arm, steered her along the busy footpath. His fingers burned where they connected with soft bare skin. Memories. Unfulfilled desire from six years ago. That was all. 'Except this is only the beginning.'

Was he mad to choose this path? He had already made sure Maria couldn't actually go bankrupt. Why not leave it at that and forget about Arabella?

Because you don't want her to get one cent out of your aunt that she hasn't worked for.

Let her squirm under his scrutiny while she worked to set things to rights. She deserved that, and he could easily control this physical awareness, even if it had taken him by surprise.

'It's just ahead.' Luc produced a set of keys from his pocket and pressed the button to disable the central locking system of the top-of-the-range sedan.

Bella's gaze followed his to look at the car. As she did so, she removed her arm from his grip. 'Good. Show me the papers.'

Controlled, instructive, as though she had any say in this.

He opened the rear door and retrieved his briefcase. '*Brique's* restaurant should be quiet. It's only another block. We'll look at the papers together.'

'Why not here? And what if I want to check that the papers are authentic?' Bella angled one hip and waited.

'If you need to check once you've looked, you can keep the papers.' Then in case she thought he would be so foolish, he said, 'Naturally, I have copies.'

He waved a hand towards his car, challenged her. 'If it suits you better to sit in the middle of this busy street...'

Bella glanced at the tinted windows of his car, seemed to size up her options. Her mouth firmed. 'I suppose *Brique's* will do.'

When they entered the restaurant, Luc ordered drinks and a platter of cheese, fruit and crackers. He considered it recompense for the use of the table, and he hadn't eaten since lunch.

'OK, so now we're in civilised surroundings.' Bella sipped her mineral water, and spread a portion of brie onto a cracker. The tremble in her hand was barely noticeable. 'If you want me to admit that you do "civilised" quite nicely, I suppose it's true. And I am hungry.'

As he was. Bella had a fiery spirit that called to something in his make-up. Luc forced himself to admit that. But he could and would control his awareness.

'I like good things.' He said it mildly enough and helped himself to brie and a cracker, too. 'I'm not ashamed of that.'

Bella ate a morsel of the food. She closed her eyes. 'Mmm. It may not be *Pont l'Eveque,* but it's nice, just the same.'

Luc snapped his briefcase open and tried not to watch the movement of her mouth, the soft lips. He spread the relevant documents out for her to view.

Bella read for a couple of minutes in silence. Then looked up, gaze narrowed. 'You say your finance manager obtained these?'

'They're the real thing, Arabella.' As real as the woman seated across the table from him, her mouth, lush, lovely, *deceptive,* pursed in a combination of suspicion, and dread.

Luc welcomed the reaction, wanted her to realise she had no control in this any more, would have to cede it to him. 'The information comes from a reputable investigative firm. As you can see, Maria's purchase of your stock was beyond risky for her.'

He indicated the cover page attached to the report. Thought about the other papers tucked safely away at home. 'You can ring the firm right now if you want. They'll confirm everything you see there.' They would once he gave them the go-ahead to reveal a certain level of information to her.

'It just can't be true.' Bella whispered the words, and bent her head again. This time she didn't come up for air until she had pored over every page. Her fingers trembled as she stacked the papers together and passed them back across the table to him.

Only then did she meet his gaze. 'But it is true, isn't it? Maria has extended herself too far to hope to climb back, and she's taken my gowns and the beginnings of my reputation as a designer with her.' Her breath faltered. 'I should have checked, shouldn't have simply assumed her financial status.

'We're both ruined. I don't see how she can even hope to recover financially, let alone allow for my gowns to be a success. My five-year plan is over before it even got started.'

'Crocodile tears, my dear?' Luc didn't buy them. He *wouldn't* buy them. He knew better than that now. Maybe Arabella hadn't confirmed Maria's financial status. That wasn't his problem, and it didn't exonerate her from pushing for the highly unreasonable deal in the first place.

'I can't buy the gowns back.' Bella's gaze dropped to her hands. She hardly seemed aware of him. 'I'm—I'm in too deep already.'

'Yet you were quite happy for Maria to be in that deep.'

'I knew it would work over time.' Unease pooled in the depths of her eyes. 'Perhaps I should have built in an escape clause for Maria.' She hesitated. 'I didn't think of her side of it.'

'You thought only to use Maria, and walk away without any responsibility if things didn't work out. Do you really believe I'll stand back and leave the future of my aunt's business in your hands now I know what you've done, Arabella?' He had bought up Maria's debts as a secret backer in order to protect her while he sorted this out with Bella. That was his business, but Bella would not be allowed to shrug off her responsibility.

'If Maria had been wealthy as I imagined...' Bella rose, stepped away from her chair and gathered her bag to her. Her movements were mechanical, but she couldn't seem to smooth them out.

Luchino believed she only wanted to use Maria. It wasn't true, but she *hadn't* considered Maria in the agreement, only herself. Bella hadn't wanted to run any risks, but Luchino wouldn't understand that, especially now!

'You *will* work with me to set things to rights, Arabella.' Luchino decreed it, like a god speaking from the peak of Mount Olympus. 'You'll wear your gowns at Melbourne's most élite functions, at the theatre and opera, in homes and at gala evenings, to dinners and parties. Anywhere your prospective clientele gather.'

'It's one thing to put on a nice dress and go to the theatre with my sisters.' They had all enjoyed such times, and nowadays the heavily pregnant Chrissy came with husband in tow and Bella *liked* Chrissy's husband, mostly, but Luc Montichelli wanted too much. 'You can't just decide this and say I have to do it. Why would you want to be with me, anyway?'

'I can say it. I can make you do it. And I don't want to be with you. I want to see to it that you comply with my demands. That my aunt doesn't suffer because of you.' His arm brushed hers as they moved out of the restaurant and stepped along the pavement. 'I want your agreement to do everything necessary to make this work, and to do it quietly and discreetly.'

'Without telling Maria about it.' Bella believed Luc's proof of Maria's financial status. She still wanted to discuss the problem with Maria. Most of all she wanted Luc to forget all this and go away. 'If I insist on speaking with Maria?'

He simply kept walking, turned that dark, exotic profile until his gaze met hers, and told her. 'If you fail in any way to comply with what I want, I will retaliate by ruining your reputation as a designer so you'll never work in that field again.'

'You would do that?' One glance into Luchino's dark, angry eyes told Bella he would. His wealth and status as an international jeweller meant he *could*.

'Don't doubt it, Arabella.' But instead of more anger at her, Luchino looked up, ahead of them, and his steps slowed.

Such an expression of anguish came over his face then that Bella almost stumbled at his side. 'Luchino? What...?'

But he didn't seem to hear her.

She followed his gaze, realised they were near his car again. Saw...a little girl and a middle-aged woman standing beside that car. A girl with curly black hair and olive skin who clung to the woman's hand while her gaze followed Luc's every movement.

Luc's daughter?

But here? With him? How? Why? Bella struggled to comprehend even the possibilities but all she saw was a scared little girl, clinging to the older woman's skirt, her face pinched and anxious as she watched Luchino's approach.

Thoughts came. Memories. Her sisters' faces had borne the same scared, confused expressions this child wore now. Over and over and over for years until Bella finally managed to rebuild enough of a life for them, enough security for them that they began to recuperate from the loss of their parents.

Bella had given her sisters all the love her parents refused to give. Had given and given it. Now her throat tightened and a stifling, smothering feeling suddenly swept over her.

'Papa?' The little girl took a few tentative steps towards them. 'You were gone a long time. Nanny Heather was scared you wouldn't come back.'

This statement brought raised eyebrows and a solemn look from the woman who stood at the child's side.

'*Grace.*' Luc murmured the child's name as though it hurt somehow to say it.

The air hummed with emotion.

'I accept your terms.' Bella blurted the words and knew she had no choice. 'I'll work to get all my gowns sold as quickly as possible, I'll attend functions with you until Maria's finances are in a better state, then I'll go on without you.' How long would it take to get to that point?

Luchino inclined his head. 'A sensible choice.'

When he started to move forward again, Bella remained where she was. 'I have to go now. I'll miss my tram. It's— it's that way.' She pointed randomly in a different direction. 'I'll be in contact about our…arrangement.'

'You don't have my number.' Luchino drew a business card from his pocket and handed it to her.

'OK. Now I have it. Goodbye.' Without waiting for his response, Bella rushed past Luc, blended into the pedestrian traffic and took the fastest possible route away from his daughter and the nanny.

CHAPTER THREE

BELLA made her way to the flat, tried to pull her emotions back under control but too much had happened too fast and she didn't know where to begin to try to come to terms with it all.

'I'm home.' She called the words out, stepped through the door, closed it and leaned on it as Soph came out of the kitchen area to greet her.

'Hi. How do you like this hair colour? It's supposed to be a rinse-out but it seems rather...' Soph stopped. 'You look like you've seen a ghost.'

'Yes.' A laugh escaped Bella and she snapped her mouth shut because it held an edge too close to hysteria to be comfortable. 'I've seen a ghost, and if I don't do what he wants he's going to take my lifelong dream from me.'

Soph peered at her for all of a second, then grabbed the cordless phone off the coffee-table and punched a speed-dial number. 'Can you come? I think we need a family council.'

'I'm fine, Sophia. There's nothing to worry about.' Bella stepped away from the door and tried to pull herself together.

But it was too late. Soph had already ended the call, and their sister arrived not long after, and Bella wasn't pulled together, anyway.

Chrissy stepped inside the flat while Bella was brewing a

pot of *chai* and trying to sort out her thoughts. Her sisters both stared at her, and Bella realised she couldn't avoid this. She would have to explain.

Maybe it would help to talk about it…

'I saw Luchino Montichelli today.' She got through two cups of tea and half a Pilates routine in her comfortable black catsuit before she finished her story with an explanation about his child. 'He—his daughter was with him. Not *with him* with him, but there, waiting by the car when we got back to it, with a nanny at her side.'

'He's taken the child back?' Soph's tone made it clear she found this incomprehensible. 'Didn't you just say he deserted her after his divorce?'

Bella fought to overcome the upsurge of pain Soph's simple question invoked. 'I find it hard to believe, too, and I have no idea if the girl is with him permanently or what. With everything else, I'd had it by then and I just left.' In fact, she had reacted in a blind panic. Bella still didn't know why she had rushed off like that!

'I wonder if he loves the child now.' Chrissy's hand caressed her distended tummy in a gentle, circling motion, but her gaze was fierce as she asked the question. 'Because a child needs to be loved and if a parent can't give it that, they have no right to even be near it.'

Soph slid her arm around Chrissy's shoulders and squeezed. 'You love your baby to bits. We all do. I can't wait to be an aunty.'

'What are you going to do, Bella?' Chrissy accepted her sister's hug, but her gaze remained fixed on Bella. 'You can't accept his ultimatum. You'd have to see him constantly, put up with his ridiculous view that you're money-hungry and used Maria.'

'I don't see that I have any choice.' Bella began to pace the floor in front of the TV.

Chrissy stepped towards her. 'Nate and I can buy your gowns back so you can leave Maria's altogether. We can set you up on your own, Bella, so you can start again. Your own shop, any location, whatever you want. I'm sure Nate would see it as a good long-term investment, and at least then you wouldn't be beholden to this Montichelli man.'

'It's either that, or the three of us all get loans for whatever the banks will lend us, and pool it to take care of the problem.' Soph nodded so that her bright pink hair flew in all directions around her face. 'That's doable as well.'

'That might work to get Bella out of Maria's.' Chrissy pushed her glasses up her pert nose as she considered Soph's suggestion. 'But I don't think we'd get enough money to set her up in a new shop. It would be rather a lot.'

'I suppose so.' Soph turned her face up and blew at a strand of hair, then looked directly at Bella. 'I guess it has to be Nate, then, and I know you and he didn't get off to a great start what with him getting Chrissy pregnant and everything, but look how well it turned out. Anyway, he'd help, and the main thing is, we don't want you back near the creep who hurt you when you were in Milan.'

'*One* of the creeps,' Chrissy reminded her. 'Remember the show manager lured Bella to his room that final night, too.'

'You should have told us the whole truth when you came back from that trip.' Soph launched into a protective tirade over the sleazy show manager's behaviour.

Chrissy added her voice to it.

Bella stood between her sisters and ached inside. She loved them. They wanted to help her but ultimately she couldn't let them. And why was it so hard to have them try to care for her?

Because the order's been reversed and you don't know how to cope with that.

'Have you told us everything now, Bella?' Chrissy's eyes behind the glasses sparked with demand for the entire truth.

'Yes, that's all of it. I know I could have told you much more about what happened in Milan at the time, but I wanted to put it behind me.' She hadn't learned of the divorce and Luc's abandonment of his child until almost a year later, either, and by then, hadn't wanted to talk about it ever again.

Now her sisters knew everything, except just how much of her heart Bella had given to Luchino in that whirlwind week overseas.

Bella drew a deep breath. 'I appreciate the offer to help me out, Chrissy, but it wouldn't be right to ask you and Nate to tie up so much money that way. It would be bucket-loads, much more than even just the cost of repurchasing the gowns, and I admit I got a good price out of Maria for them.' When she named the figure, both sisters gasped.

Bella shrugged. 'I put every spare cent into creating that stock of gowns, and they *are* designer-wear.'

She hesitated as she considered her situation, and then admitted in a low tone, 'Right now I'm wondering if I should have given up modelling. It's true it was never my dream job, but maybe I miscalculated the risks in branching out into fashion. Just because I've created all our clothes for years—'

'You've created the most amazing outfits on a shoestring budget. Anything from jeans to stunning stuff fit to wear to a palace. You have the talent, Bella,' Chrissy insisted.

And Bella remembered that even Luchino admitted she had ability. She had to believe that, too. Now was not the time to doubt! Bella held Chrissy's gaze. 'I can't let you and Soph get loans to help me, either, although I appreciate both thoughts very much.'

'But you have to get out.' This came from Soph.

'No. Luchino said I have no choice, and he's right. I have to sell the gowns quickly. If working with Luchino is the only way to do that—' she shrugged '—I'll have to cope, that's all.'

'It will fix the problem.' Chrissy gave a reluctant nod. 'Provided he doesn't try to encroach on the business arrangement, make it more personal or anything.' She gave Bella a searching look. 'Is that likely to happen?'

'Not when he thinks I'm money-hungry, and when I know all he is capable of. Distrust on both sides is not fertile ground for the development of anything personal.' Refusing to think of the twinges of awareness that had passed between her and Luchino, Bella hugged first one sister, then the other, being careful not to squash Chrissy's baby bump in the process. 'Thanks for the talk and for what you both offered to do to help.'

'What—what about his daughter?' It was Soph who asked the question, who tried hard to hide her vulnerability as she waited for the answer. 'Maybe we should, you know, look into how he's treating her or something.'

'Oh, Soph.' Bella had wrestled with that very question five years ago but what could some upstart twenty-year-old do from another country when a multimillionaire chose to leave his child in what was probably thoroughly adequate care while he ignored said child? Who would have even listened to her concerns?

But she was wrestling with those same concerns again now and knew she had to act on them. It was the right thing to do even if she now suspected it was also the reason for her earlier panic. She would have to remain at an emotional distance, that was all. 'I'll look into it, Soph.'

In fact, this was how Bella had to tackle the whole situation. She would do what she had to, but her emotions would remain safely behind those fortified walls around her heart.

'I can do this. It'll work out. I'll take care of myself and make sure I can't get hurt.'

'If you get out of your depth, you *will* let us get you out of there.' Chrissy decreed it.

Bella reluctantly nodded, even though she had no intention of allowing her sisters or brother-in-law to cough up that kind of money no matter what.

'All right, then I guess we're settled. And I want to show Danni and Michelle this hair colour.' Soph headed for her bedroom. 'I'd better see what I've got to wear tonight.'

Once both her sisters were gone, Chrissy to the home she made with Nate Barrett and Sophia to a club with her girl-friends, Bella took the business card Luchino had pressed on her as she escaped him near his car earlier, and phoned the after-hours number.

'Montichelli.' Even the sound of his voice over the phone cut a swathe through her nervous system.

So get over it. It's just a voice.

'I want an itinerary of events you expect me to attend with you so I can work out what to wear for each occasion.' She didn't bother with a greeting, just launched into the purpose of her call. Which was to arm herself with information, and to take as much control as she could over the situation. 'I'll agree not to say anything to your aunt about it for now, but I want it on record that I don't like the deceit. When will we go to our first event?'

'Tomorrow evening.' He named the hosts and the suburb they lived in. 'They're a husband and wife who own a chain of member-only golf courses around the country. I'll call for you at seven.'

'I'd also like to know how you intend to explain these outings to your aunt—' Bella stopped abruptly, because Luc had handed down his order, and ended the call!

* * *

Bella thought back over that conversation as she put the finishing touches to her make-up the next night. Or rather, she thought about the things she should have asked, but hadn't got a chance to. It was Saturday, and she wished it was Saturday a year from now and Luchino Montichelli was once again a distant memory. How long *would* it take to rid herself of him?

Soph stood in the open doorway of the bathroom, one hand wrapped around the door frame, a hairbrush in the other. The pink hair had washed out, Bella noted with affection. The outcome had been touch-and-go for a while there for her funky hairdresser sister.

'It's not too late to change your mind about this, Bella. Luchino Montichelli has no right to make you do this stuff.'

'He's concerned about his aunt.' Bella didn't say it to try to placate Soph. Rather, she had pondered it and decided Luchino really did seem to care about her boss.

'And you're going to check on his daughter.' At that pronouncement, Soph relaxed a little.

Bella, on the other hand, stiffened before she managed to force a smile. 'Yes. I'll do what I can. And Soph, I have no interest in being close to Luchino in any way but a business one.'

Probably when Luchino arrived tonight, Bella would feel nothing at all towards him except irritation that she had to be in his presence. The earlier internal twitters would simply have been a result of memories and the shock of seeing him suddenly after so long. She had schooled herself now.

'If you say so.' In the past, her sisters would have simply accepted her assurance, but Soph didn't look completely convinced. 'Chrissy and I still don't like that this man insists you go out with him under the guise of business. What if he tries to seduce you again?' Her voice filled with concern. 'We don't want him to hurt you.'

'I won't let him, and you and Chrissy should worry about

your own issues, not mine. I shouldn't have told you so much.' But her sisters rarely had 'issues' any more, and somehow that knowledge left Bella feeling rather lost, confused when her sisters tried to watch over her, upset when she no longer had the chance to watch over them.

Anyway, you're not lost. You have a whole new career to pursue.

One that was now the source of a great deal of concern for her.

With one final glance at herself, Bella twitched the midnight-blue gown into place and hustled Sophia out into the living room. 'It's just business, Soph. All I need to do is treat it as such.'

Footsteps sounded outside, followed by a sharp rap on the door.

Bella's heart stumbled in a way she couldn't blame on irritation or unease. But it wasn't awareness, either, because she had talked herself out of any more of that nonsense. She moved towards the door on four-inch stiletto heels and warned her sister over her shoulder, 'Leave this to me.'

On those words, Bella pulled the door open, and tried not to notice the devastation that was Luchino Montichelli in full evening garb. She drew a deep breath.

He looks nice. There's nothing personal in noticing.

'Hello, Luchino.' *Catch that calm tone? This is me, Luchino, ignoring you on every level but that of business acquaintance.* 'I'm ready to leave.'

'Good evening, Arabella. Won't you introduce me?' Luc glanced beyond her shoulder and stepped into the flat's small living room before Bella fully realised his intention.

Great, now she got to sense him as well as see him, and he smelled nice, too, like freshly showered man. Not that she cared what he smelled like. 'Uh—'

'Bella?' Soph fingered the hairbrush clutched in her right hand and looked at Luc through narrowed eyes.

Soph's intervention brought Bella out of her...momentary surprise, or whatever this was. Bella stiffened her spine, took two sensible steps away from Luchino.

'Sophia, meet Luchino. Luchino, my sister Sophia.' She rattled the introductions off as she sent a quelling stare in Soph's direction, then turned back to Luc. She wasn't about to dwell on the introductions, nor give her sister time to start an inquisition that would only waste time.

'Let's go.' She wanted Luchino out of here, wanted to start this evening because once she started it, she was on the way to ending it. 'We have some matters to discuss on the way to the dinner ball. You terminated our phone conversation without allowing me to finish my questions.'

'So eager for my company, Arabella?' Luc's gaze clashed with hers. He examined her, head to toe and back again, from beneath lowered lids. When he met her gaze once more, a flicker of awareness showed in his eyes. He quickly masked the reaction but it was enough to make her breath catch with...unease and...annoyance at him.

While she drew a steadying breath, Luc spoke again. 'You look...good.'

'Thank you. I, um...' She had to pull herself together! She would start by making it clear what she expected of tonight, and her whole association with him. 'I'm certainly not eager for your company, as you suggested a moment ago. Some things just have to be endured and are best over with quickly. Like when you have to swallow a nasty-tasting medicine.'

'That's how you envision our evening?' His mouth twitched, but quickly firmed.

'It's how I envisage all of this, until it finally ends.' There. Let him chew on that.

She broke the hold of his gaze and yanked the apartment door open. 'If we're quite finished with the chit-chat, perhaps we could go.'

Luchino turned his attention briefly to their surroundings, and then approached the flat's front door and stood back for Bella to precede him through it. 'By all means. The evening awaits us.'

He cast a final glance at Sophia, whom Bella had completely forgotten in the few short moments that had just passed. 'It was nice to meet you. Perhaps we'll have a chance to speak more another day.'

'We'll see!' The hairbrush quivered in Soph's hand.

Bella eyed her sister cautiously. Next thing Soph would be brandishing the brush at Luc, threatening death by bristle attack if he didn't behave. 'We're *fine*, Sophia, just a couple of small issues that needed airing. Sorry if we left you out of the conversation.'

Smile. Glide out of the door. Let the smile fade.

Once on the road, Luc guided his car through the traffic with no apparent effort. The scent of leather seats and his cologne pressed in on Bella's senses and dulled them until she realised what was happening and stiffened her spine.

'Your sister seems nice.' Luc made the observation in a neutral tone. 'A little protective, maybe.'

So Luc had noticed the hairbrush, too. Bella's unease softened a little at the thought of her youngest sister. 'Soph's a hairdresser.' As though that explained everything, when in fact it explained nothing at all.

Anyway, this wasn't about that. Bella had questions. She wanted answers. 'You haven't said how we're supposed to explain all this to your aunt.' Bella wanted to know what he was thinking, planning. 'Us working together to sell my gowns, I mean. If we start to get the kind of notice you hope for, won't Maria wonder why we're out at all those functions together?'

'We can take care of that problem.' He merged for a right turn and, as they waited for a green light, drew some folded pages from his breast pocket and passed them to her. 'That's the itinerary to date. I'll let you know of any changes or additions as they happen.'

'At a glance it all looks...acceptable.' She recognised some of the names on his list, and knew she would never have got near those people.

But she didn't have to feel grateful. Bella stuffed the list of functions and explanations into her evening bag. Against the carpeted floor of the car, she tapped the foot of one stiletto. 'You haven't addressed my question.'

He shrugged the broad shoulders that looked so brilliant under jet-black dinner suiting. 'We tell my aunt as much truth as we can. We knew each other years ago in Milan. When I came back to Australia, we renewed the acquaintance. Now we're having fun going out together.'

'You want us to act like we're dating?' Her question hung in the air in shocked denial.

'It will save a lot of awkward questions.' Luc's face was impassive, blank, yet somehow Bella sensed he wasn't as withdrawn from this as he made out. He went on. 'I think we can manage a credible image of two people very interested in each other. Don't you?'

Her heart skipped a beat. In fury at his audacity! 'Just because we once had a brief relationship...' She wished the traffic lights would turn green so Luc would stop looking at her. 'We can't pretend to be lovers.'

The lights changed and the car moved forward. When Luc responded, it was with a tinge of challenge in his tone. 'I don't recall using the term lovers, but we need a reason to be seen together, to be in the public eye together so much. Is it such a big deal to you, Arabella? Surely, if it keeps Maria happy and you sell your gowns—'

'You should just tell her the truth.'

'She's my family. I won't let anything happen to her. I've already taken steps—' He swore and cut himself off.

But it was too late. Because Bella remembered a previous hesitation when he'd said 'I don't want her to know I bought—' and now those words made sense. Bella turned her head, looked right at the dark, handsome face. 'You bought up her debts, didn't you? But if you've done that, why bother with me about it? It's taken care of, isn't it?'

'Except for the fact that *you're* responsible for getting all that money back in for your gowns, and I intend to see that you do it! How did you guess, anyway? I haven't said I've done anything.' His hands tightened on the wheel as he muttered the words.

Bella looked at the long, tanned fingers and remembered them cupping her chin, a preparation for kissing her.

No! That had been years ago. This was now and she had nothing but dislike for him. 'It was just something you almost said.' She brushed that off. 'How much was it, Luchino? What are the terms? How much does Maria owe you?'

He made a frustrated sound in the back of his throat. 'It doesn't matter how I did it, or how much or how little. I couldn't leave her dangling like that so I…made arrangements.'

'It matters to me.' Bella felt as though one more revelation might crack her completely in two. 'I sold my stock to *Maria*, not to you.' That was the crux of her concern. Oh, that mattered! 'I don't want to be financially tied to you.'

'Don't you? Well, you've just given me a reason to answer you.' Anger flared in his tone and he went on ruthlessly. 'I bought up Maria's debts and arranged for her to pay the money back at a low rate of interest on a long-term repayment plan.

'As far as she's concerned, it's an almost philanthropic gesture from someone who wishes to feel part of the fashion industry, has money to invest any way he likes and is eccentric enough to do something like this just for his own pleasure. I guess *I own you now,* Arabella. Get used to it.'

'You've become a silent backer.' Even though she had expected the truth to be unpalatable, lead formed in the pit of Bella's stomach. No doubt he only told her to make her feel even worse.

'When Maria's ready for it, I'll tell her the whole truth.' He sent a glance towards Bella. Let her see the warning in his eyes. 'Until then, you won't speak of this to her. I have to work things out for her in the way I believe is best.'

'You've made it impossible for me to speak to her,' Bella fumed, 'as you well know!'

'Maria's welfare is what matters to me in all of this.' He cast another quick glance at her, and made a lightning change of subject. 'You never spoke of your family when we were in Milan together, yet I see you must be close to your sisters. You have a wall full of photos of the three of you, and Sophia is clearly protective of you, but what of your parents?'

That one short moment inside her apartment, and he had missed nothing.

'Roaming the galaxies in outer space for all I know.' The words snapped out of her. She stopped and forced herself to take a deep breath. 'My sisters are what matter to me.'

Luc swung the car onto a wide tree-lined boulevard style of street. For the past few minutes, the houses had become larger, better, more prestigious. They stopped before the biggest of them all. Cars lined the long, sweeping driveway and a substantial part of the street.

'You've had a falling-out with your parents?' He seemed almost troubled, but clearly she must be imagining that!

No, Luchino, they left us, just like you left your daughter years ago.

'We're here. Let's get this over with.' Bella got out of the car and started up the long drive towards the suburban mansion. She didn't want to discuss her personal life with him.

The ornate double doors of the home loomed in front of them. At the sight, her nerves hiked. She lifted her chin as they approached the doors, took in a careful breath. Drew on the inner reserves she relied on to get her through any challenge.

Luc's eyes narrowed. 'It's your armour. For when you're scared.' He gave a self-directed laugh. 'Why didn't I see that before now? Your chin goes up, you withdraw into some place that makes others believe you're so sufficient in and of yourself you couldn't need anything else, but it's all just a veil for your uncertainty.'

'I want to succeed. That's all.' She hated that he could see through what most of the rest of the world had never seen at all, hated that he knew her unease. To make up for that fact, she glared at him.

'Good evening. May I take your things?' The sonorous tones came from a very elegant-looking man in full butler's attire.

They were quickly ushered into a formal ballroom area with an ornate chandelier in the high-domed ceiling, and a lot of glitzy, ritzy, very expensive-looking people who milled about in a studied, elegant throng.

Panic rose. 'Wait…'

Luc could have played on that nervous feeling. Instead, he threw her off guard by giving her an encouraging glance. 'They're just people. It'll be fine.'

His hand against the bare flesh of her shoulders guided her forward. When he bent his head to whisper lightly into her ear,

Bella struggled to comprehend his words, because most of her senses were attuned only to his nearness and that was so wrong. She raised her head and promised herself she wouldn't sense another thing about him all night.

'Come on.' If he noticed her preoccupation, he gave no indication of it. Instead, he gestured towards the clusters of people gathered beyond them. 'Let's see you convince these women they want to wear your gowns.'

Bella lifted her chin and did her best to quell the nerves made all the more edgy by Luc's touch. 'I'm more than willing to court the attention of the women here tonight, to interest them in my gowns.' Bella spoke in the strongest tone she could manage. 'I want to set things to rights as quickly as I can so I no longer have to see you!'

Luc simply smiled in that devastating way he had that made her want to smack him. Or run away. Maybe both.

'Then let's mingle,' he said. 'Shall we?'

CHAPTER FOUR

'YOU seem to be making a positive impression on the guests.' Since the start of the evening, Luc had kept Bella tucked against his side. He did it to watch her, to make sure she made every effort to attract interest in her gowns. But she attracted his interest, too.

What was it about Arabella Gable that held him despite their past, despite their current situation? He had plenty of reasons to steer clear of her, yet he couldn't put her out of his thoughts, couldn't deny his awareness of her.

You sought her out, forced her into this.

He ignored the thought. Arabella had played his aunt an unfair hand and she had to pay the cost of her actions. That was all. Even so, she roused his curiosity. What about her parents, for example? She must have had a falling-out with them or something. 'For your sake I hope that impression leads to gown sales in the near future.'

'I hope for that, too.' Her eyes caught the colour of her dress. The hint of dark blue in the brown depths lent her an air of mystery. The sparks of irritation were clear. 'As I said, I'm all for parting company with you as soon as possible, Luchino.'

'But you can't part company with me just yet, because you need me to help you gain entrée to functions like this one.'

He watched frustration fill her and threaten to bubble over. Something deep within him *wanted* her to lose her control, to fly at him, let all her feelings loose.

Dinner was announced, Bella dropped her gaze and Luc reluctantly turned his attention to finding their places at the long oval table. Sparring with her stimulated him, as did her nearness. He shouldn't allow those reactions.

At the dinner table Bella talked, schmoozed, shone like a bright light, all of it directed away from Luc, but he *felt* each word she spoke, each dazzling smile she directed anywhere but at him.

If he kissed her, tasted her lips, would this curious interest in her, this humming awareness, be satisfied and disappear?

When the butler lit hundreds of candles in the shimmering ballroom and an orchestral trio began to play, Luc guided her into the room with his mind on those questions. Maybe a dance would give him his answer.

'Let's dance. An attractive woman in a beautiful gown, moving to the music—what could appeal more?' He drew her onto the dance floor, enjoyed the flare of startled awareness that rose in her eyes. 'Can you sell your name and your merchandise this way, Arabella?'

'I can do whatever I have to.' The strains of a waltz began. Strain coloured her words, too, but she took up his challenge.

He swept her into the dance. Their bodies moved in perfect harmony. She fitted as though she belonged in his arms and, while awareness began a slow burn along his nerve-endings, he hadn't anticipated the sense of rightness that came from holding her this way.

Bella was silent, but soft colour flushed her cheeks, and her eyes shone.

Other couples glided around the floor but Luc only saw Bella, and he sensed she only saw him.

His grip tightened, he swung Bella into a turn and kept her close, allowed the dance to become something more because right at this moment the dance had her. Luc had her, he knew it, and acknowledged the surge of power and demand that came with that understanding. He wanted to take her to bed, to spend the night in physical passion with her.

'This dance is finished. The evening is finished.' He stopped, clasped her hand in his and tugged her across the floor. The final strains of the music coincided.

To an onlooker, they simply left the floor at the zenith of the dance, a fitting end to a perfect performance, but they both knew otherwise.

'Luc?' Bella moved along at his side. She tried to pull her fingers from his grip. 'Wh-what are you doing? I could dance with some other people, mingle—'

'Not tonight.' He maintained his clasp on her hand. 'You and I have unfinished business that needs to be laid to rest once and for all.'

It almost sounded rational, but for the fact that he dragged her straight past their hostess and out into the hall, where the butler appeared and handed Bella her wrap. Their host also appeared.

That should have steadied Luc, even if only a little. Instead he waited impatiently while the other man said his goodbyes. When the guy took Bella's hand and kissed it, Luc stepped forward. A silent warning growled low in his being.

'Yes, well, good evening and thank you for attending.' The man stepped back, away from Arabella, away from Luc's glare that insisted he do so.

Luc muttered something that might or might not have been appropriate in response, and finally they were free of the place. They started down the long driveway, side by side, his hand at Bella's back to guide her.

Cool night air brushed against Luc's face, neck, hands. He felt only the burn of desire.

'Luc?' Her gaze sought his, searched. 'I'm not sure what you're thinking, but I really don't feel we can go on—'

'This way?' They reached the car. Luc caged her against the side of it, not touching, but close—very close. 'You want me. I can see it in your eyes.'

Bella pressed back against the passenger door. Her brown eyes widened. 'What makes you believe that? I haven't said anything.'

'This is what makes me believe it, Arabella, just this.' He swooped, covered her mouth with his. In the kiss he would lay the questions to rest, and then he would set that hunger aside for all time.

Except her lips were soft and responsive, and tasted of things he hadn't realised he wanted, but now he did. She gasped at the shock of first contact, and he took advantage of that soft sound to taste her. He should have drawn back then, when the need to quench the questions became a need for more. But he didn't.

Instead, he cupped her shoulders and let their mouths relearn each other, caress each other, while his heart thundered and he wondered if he knew what he was doing, at all.

Although slender, she was soft. So soft, everywhere he touched. That softness contrasted to the strong, determined woman she presented to the world. Luc thought this, and realised he had somehow allowed Arabella to get inside his thoughts, to stir up feelings inside him, to make him want her in more than just a physical sense.

That realisation made him break the kiss, step back, put distance between them. It wasn't supposed to end up like this, and how *could* it feel special or anything else of note, when he knew what she was like?

No. It was an unanticipated attack of sexual desire. That was all. Anything else he had simply imagined.

Bella stared at him, eyes dilated, mouth soft and swollen. She seemed stunned, too, but she spoke quickly, her gaze not quite meeting his. 'That shouldn't have happened.'

'Don't put too much store by the kiss, Arabella. I felt we should put old ghosts to rest, that's all.' Yet he wanted her to admit he had stirred her. Why? Because he wanted to punish her for what had happened back then, and for trying to take advantage of his aunt now? Quite possibly.

Her mouth tightened and the luminous quality in her eyes changed to an expression of rejection. 'You were a married man. I worked hard to forget you once I found that out.'

Luc could have told her he had been separated, that he had planned to tell her his situation and ask her to understand. He didn't. Why give Arabella that knowledge to maybe use against him?

Bella drew herself to her full height. 'So you wanted to bury any feelings or attraction we may have felt in the past. Consider that done and don't ever kiss me again.'

She raised the whispery wrap from her elbows, spread it across her shoulders and clasped its ends in front of her. A filigree shield that did nothing to protect her from him or from what had happened here.

'The kiss served its purpose. I see no reason to repeat it.' Yet even as he tossed this at her, Luc's body hummed with the wish to draw her back, to explore further with her. He clamped his teeth together and assured himself this *had* addressed their history. Now they could go forward in the way he wanted. Bella would work to sell her gowns, and he would watch to make sure she did it, and that was all. He wanted control over her behaviour, not closeness to her.

A taxi turned into the end of the street, drew to a halt some distance away to dispense its passengers outside a stately house, and moved on towards Luc and Bella.

Before she raised her arm, Luc guessed her intention.

'I'll call for you tomorrow at six for the cruise dinner on the Yarra River.' He dropped his gaze to her feet, to toenails painted a pale, seductive pink. 'Be careful to wear footwear you can manage on a moving deck.'

'I intend to be careful around you in every way there is, Luchino, starting right now.' She climbed into the back of the taxi, gave her directions, and as the cab swept into the darkness she didn't look back.

Luc got in his car, drove to his house, and when he got inside he checked on his sleeping daughter. The nanny, Heather, would be asleep in the room next to Grace's, where she stayed any time Luc said he would be late home.

Grace…

She looked so much like Dominic when she slept. Luc bent to brush a kiss across Grace's forehead and a burst of protectiveness swept over him.

How could he have walked away from her? It was a pain he would live with forever.

He sighed and went on to his own room. On Monday Maria would be back in her store. Even now she might be home, might have played his phone message. If she didn't respond over the weekend, he would go to the store on Monday.

Yes. He would focus on Maria, on getting to know her, and keep Bella at arm's length in all but the necessary dealings.

They saw Melbourne by water on a luxury flybridge cruiser that held back nothing in terms of self-indulgence for its hand-picked guests. Waiters circulated with platters of tiny rounds of minced lamb stuffed with green olives, or squid and chorizo skewers and exotic frittatas that melted on the tongue.

After one vodka fruitini Bella switched to mineral water. Luc drank a rich red wine the colour of the silk shirt he wore. As night-time fell, the city became an endless view of glittering lights and beautiful buildings and lush gardens both private and public. It was wonderfully romantic, and Bella mingled with the guests and talked shop and held herself aloof from Luchino because romantic was not on her agenda or his, and she had to remember that.

When the evening ended she drew a deep, relieved breath, hailed another taxi—her choice, and Luc would simply have to accept that—and tried not to notice the way the night breeze ruffled his dark hair, nor how the angles and planes of his face seemed to fill with sensual secrets in the semi-darkness.

'Goodnight.' She said it firmly as she stepped into the cab. 'I'll see you for our next event together.'

And I will not think about you or *anticipate* seeing you, until that time.

She survived relatively unscathed in her 'not thinking of Luchino' world until halfway through Monday, when his voice disturbed the momentary quiet of the shop.

'I know you won't remember me, Zia. I don't remember you, either, but I'd like to get to know you.'

Bella's head snapped up and the needle in her hand poked through the fabric at an odd angle. But it was his *tone* that made her sit very still as she waited to hear Maria's response.

Luc had sounded both tentative and hopeful, as though this meeting mattered to him a great deal and he really didn't know whether Maria would accept him into her life or not. Bella suffered an unwanted spurt of empathetic concern, perhaps because this was a family issue, and family in the form of her sisters meant so much to her.

At the thought of her sisters, Bella's conscience pricked her because she hadn't done anything more about Luc's daughter as yet, either. It was one thing to tell her sisters she would look into the little girl's welfare, but how did she go about that and keep as much distance from Luc as she could?

When Bella heard no response to Luc's words, just a stretch of silence, she leaned a little to the left until she could see him around the racks of gowns in the shop. He stood on the customer side of the service counter, in profile to her. She hadn't studied his profile, really, and…it looked as good as all his other angles.

Her gaze moved on to Maria, and Bella stifled a startled gasp. Her employer's face was ashen. Maria looked haunted and her lips moved silently as her gaze locked on Luc's face.

'Maria?' Bella didn't stop to think. She simply got up and moved towards her employer to help her.

At the sound of her voice, Luc glanced her way. The flash of helplessness on his face before he masked it made Bella's heart inexplicably squeeze.

'Oh, Arabella, I forgot you were working over there.' Maria flapped a hand, but didn't seem to know what to say next.

Bella did her best to put the older woman at ease. 'I just thought I'd see if everything's OK here?'

'Yes. That is, I don't know. Oh, I hadn't expected this, you see, although perhaps I should have—' Maria cut herself off and peered helplessly at Bella.

'You're surprised to meet Luchino.' It was just his name, but somehow the word had the power to shorten her breath. It wasn't fair.

What had happened to all her resolve and resistance? It had got her through the river cruise well enough.

Yes, if you don't count the dozen times you fell into a daydream about dancing across the deck in his arms.

Luc was a good dancer. That was all.

And the kiss? You haven't thought of that, imagined kissing him again?

Oh, shut up!

A movement beyond Luc's tall, lean form drew Bella's gaze. His daughter stood at his side. The little girl stared with rounded eyes at the merchandise in the store, her fingers clasped in her father's, and that simple hand-clasp made Bella's heart dip with a combination of hope and wariness.

Did Luc love his child? If so, how could he have left her? But Luc *had* left his child and he was a cheat and there were ramifications of that. People got hurt in the process and those hurts stayed with them forever.

Are you thinking about his daughter, or about yourself and your sisters?

She was thinking of both, and there was nothing wrong with that!

'Arabella, you're just in time to hear my invitation and to meet my daughter.' In the face of Maria's frozen reaction, Luc turned a suave smile in Bella's direction, but tension bracketed his mouth as he went on. 'Grace, this is Arabella Gable.'

Right. A chance to meet Luc's daughter. Good. That was good. Bella didn't feel suddenly threatened, herself. No. She felt calm and in control and one hundred per cent able to handle this. 'Hello, Grace. It's nice to meet you.'

The words came out, but her voice was husky and a tight, achy feeling filled her chest.

The little girl examined Bella for a long moment before she gave a small nod, and a shy and perhaps hopeful smile. 'Hello. It's nice to meet you, too.'

Bella warned her heart not to melt. But everything about the little girl appealed. Grace's words bore more of an accent than Luc's, and a slight lisp came as she spoke through the gaps left by missing baby teeth at the front of the small, rosebud mouth. How could she be anything but adorable and how could Bella do anything but react to that?

'Well done, Grace.' Luc's hand came to rest on his daughter's shiny dark hair.

It was a caress any father would bestow on his child, but the sight touched Bella in an even more threatening way because it told Bella that Luc *did* care.

Yet when Bella glanced at Grace, she saw the half-hopeful, half-afraid expression on her face, and hurt and hope and confusion in her liquid brown eyes. His daughter was unhappy.

It was Maria who broke into Bella's thoughts.

'Luchino, and with a daughter of your own.' The older woman's gaze clung to Luc's face as though now she had him before her she didn't want to lose even a moment by looking away. 'I—I knew you were in Melbourne, that you'd started a store here, and I got your phone message. I didn't know...I wanted—I wasn't sure if I should—'

'You didn't know what to expect of me?' Luc's shrug appeared deliberately casual.

Could he see how much this meeting appeared to mean to Maria, even if the older woman looked shaken? Whatever had taken her away from her family, Maria seemed to want to soak up the sight of this particular member of it now. Hope and uncertainty, longing and unease warred on her face.

'I'm aware you haven't seen any of the family for a long time. I won't ask you to explain that.' His gentle tone underlined that assurance far more forcefully than anything else could have, and Bella knew he had, indeed, understood very well.

Luc went on in that same calm voice, yet now counterbalanced with what *he* wanted, too. 'I simply hoped you might make an exception for me and come to dinner at my home. I'd like the chance to get to know you, and for Grace to know her aunt in Melbourne, too.'

'Oh; oh, my.' Maria's hands twisted in front of her.

Luc stepped closer to the counter, closer to Bella at the same time. Before she could consider stepping back, he gripped her hand.

'I'm not sure if Bella's mentioned it, but she and I are seeing each other.' His low words filled Maria's silence in an obvious effort to give her a moment to collect herself. 'We first met in Milan years ago and we've renewed our acquaintance since I came to Australia.'

Out came the story to cover the appearances they would make at various functions. Bella felt doubly guilty about deceiving Maria, but the older woman simply turned a distracted smile in Bella's direction.

'That's—how delightful, my dear.'

'We're really just friends, Maria.' Bella spoke without thought to the consequences. 'But I'm very pleased you and Luchino have met up again after so long.'

'Is that what you call it, Arabella? Friendship between us?' Luc's calm challenge came with a sensual curve of his lips and a very direct look into Bella's eyes that made her feel as though he could see all the way to her soul. That look was for Maria's benefit. But his gaze held a warning, too.

He leaned forward, as though to nuzzle the curve of Bella's neck. But his whispered words were far from lover-like.

'Stick by the agreement, Arabella, or suffer the consequences of breaking it.' His lips pressed for just a moment to the sensitive cord of her neck before he straightened and turned to smile at Maria. 'Please say you'll come to dinner with us tonight, Zia. It would mean a lot to us.'

'I will come. Thank you for the invitation.' Maria seemed surprised by her own answer, almost frightened by it, but she quickly turned to Bella. 'Arabella can bring me in her little car, so I don't worry about getting lost.'

'Ah…' It was Bella's week to have first call on the car. Now that Chrissy's husband had bought her a sporty convertible, dark blue with headlamps that looked like sleepy eyes, Bella and Sophia had joint possession of Gertie, the elderly yellow bug.

Normally, Bella would be glad to drive Maria anywhere she liked, but she didn't want to get dragged into this intimate dinner with Luc and his daughter and aunt. 'That's a nice idea, Maria, but I don't—'

'Don't intend to drink and drive?' Luc intercepted her smoothly and gave an approving nod. 'Very sensible. I promise I'll have something nice on the table that's non-alcoholic.'

Bella glanced from Luchino to Maria. Now that his aunt believed they were a couple, she clearly expected Bella to attend the dinner, too. Blast Luchino anyway!

'I'll be happy to be there, of course.' She pushed the words through her teeth and forced a smile. But perhaps the night wouldn't be wasted. There might be a chance to question the nanny and get some assurance about the child, or even just observe the little girl in her home environment.

If Luc was taking care of her, then Bella could tell her sisters so and they would no doubt agree there was nothing more to be done. Though Bella would never forgive his past behaviour.

Meanwhile, Luc put out a general air of satisfaction now that he had Maria's agreement to go to dinner at his house, and hastened to seal the deal by smiling in Bella's direction. 'I'll do my best to make sure you enjoy the night, Bella *mia*.'

His Bella?

Not in this lifetime. Bella turned her head so Maria wouldn't see her glare, opened her mouth to speak, to put Luchino in his place, but he spoke first.

'Seven pm at my house.' He made use of the notepad on the service counter to scribble an address, and pressed the piece of paper into her palm.

The touch of his fingers sent little shock waves radiating outward from the centre of her hand. Bella's fingers closed around the paper, around that tingling sensation caused simply by the touch of his hand.

With a slight bow at the waist, Luc smiled at his aunt. 'I look forward to welcoming you into my home. Thank you for agreeing to come to dinner.'

'I barely deserve—' But Maria cut herself off.

A customer entered the shop. Luchino glanced toward the young woman, then gave a slight nod to Maria and Bella, and, with Grace's hand still firmly clasped in his own, he left the store.

Bella wanted to ask Maria what she had started to say. One glance at the woman's now closed face let her know her questions would not be welcomed. Instead, Bella turned her attention to the customer. When she recognised the woman as a guest from the dinner ball, anticipation shimmied down her spine.

A prospective sale?

'I'm sure I can leave you to attend this lady, Arabella.' Maria's words were soft, professional, but her eyes were haunted as she collected her bag from beneath the counter and turned towards the door. 'I…need a moment to myself.'

Bella watched the older lady walk away, and yet more questions filled her mind. Why was Maria so shaken from the encounter with her nephew?

Hannah, the shop assistant, was still dressing mannequins at the far rear of the store. Bella glided forward to the customer with a determined smile. 'Hello. How may I help you?'

CHAPTER FIVE

THE doorbell chimed. Luc drew a deep breath and realised he felt...nervous. He wanted Maria to like him and want to be part of his life. It meant more to him than it maybe should have, but from the moment he'd looked into her eyes he had felt a connection.

He couldn't explain it, but it was there. When he pulled open the door, Maria stood before it, twisting the straps of a black handbag, and yes, that same feeling washed through him. Luc smiled and wished she didn't appear so nervous of his presence. 'Welcome to my home. Please, come in.'

Bella stood to the side beyond Maria. As he opened the door wider, he saw Bella fully. She wore a simple sleeveless dress of a deep sage-green. It reached to just above her knees and made him realise how tall and slender she was. Her legs seemed to go on forever, and inspired thoughts in him that were not appropriate with his aunt standing right beside them.

'Bella.' Her name emerged in a tone far too deep and not at all casual and uninterested. Luc cleared his throat and spoke again. 'Come inside.'

Bella looked into Luchino's dark, beautiful eyes and warned herself not to show any sign of awareness. But his desire to befriend his aunt, his gentleness towards Maria and towards his daughter, undermined the clear-cut nature of Bella's opinions of him and that left her vulnerable.

She mustn't forget all he had done. If she did, she might fall prey to the way he made her feel, and become vulnerable to him. She might even fall for him again. The thought made her raise her chin in sharp rejection.

'Good evening, Luch—*Luc.*' No doubt Maria would find it odd if Bella went around calling him by his full name, yet Bella missed the distancing effect it afforded her. 'Here we are, as…agreed.' It was more like him forcing her to attend. Bella stepped forward. She had some vain hope of passing him, of moving into the house and keeping a sensible half-a-room of distance between them from that point on.

Luc didn't let her pass.

'Arabella, you look ravishing.' He wrapped his hands around her upper arms and kissed each cheek and it was so Mediterranean, so Luchino, so shivery and nice that she simply stood there and let him grip her arms and smile into her eyes while sparks of awareness danced in the backs of his dark brown orbs.

And then he leaned in to place a swift kiss on her mouth. Swift, but sensual, and Bella lost even more ground.

When they separated and she glanced again into his face, she saw the effects of the kiss there, too, and suspected he had also been taken by surprise. 'I—you can't—I told you I don't want—'

'And Maria.' Luc ignored Bella's disjointed protests, gave his aunt the same salute on each cheek, and stood back so they could come inside.

Inexplicably, when Bella stepped into Luchino's home, she felt as though she could belong here. It was an impossible thought, not only because of Luc's ruthless interference in her business life, but also because of his history with his daughter. 'Luc. It's a pleasure to be here to *help you get to know your aunt.*'

With her eyes, Bella warned that she expected Luc to stick to a businesslike attitude this evening between them. Heat fired in his expression in response, but after a moment he gave an imperceptible nod.

He agreed with her. The kiss really had only been for Maria's benefit. Well, that was great. *Great.*

So where was the huge sense of relief Bella should now feel?

Before she could regain her equilibrium, Luc turned to Maria. 'Dinner will be ready in a few moments. Come and meet Heather, who is our housekeeper and nanny.'

The house was large but it had an aura of comfort, the furniture expensive leather and polished wood, but functional and lived-in. Throw rugs covered the floors in gaily patterned scatters.

A large vase of assorted flowers in wildly clashing colours stood on the dining table, arranged haphazardly. Bella turned her gaze and found Luc's attention focused on her.

Not wanting him to sense her confusion, she forced a smile. 'Are the flowers from your garden?'

'Yes.' For a moment, his contained expression faltered. 'Grace and Heather picked the flowers and "arranged" them.'

'Well, they're beautiful.' This came from Maria, but nerves coloured her tone.

A look passed between nephew and aunt that Bella couldn't quite fathom. They both seemed to be searching for something in the other.

When they entered the kitchen, they found Grace on a high stool, skinny legs dangling as she meticulously cut out rounds of pastry with a cutter in the shape of a kangaroo. Flour dusted the counter in front of her, the floor around her and quite a bit of the bib apron she wore over a frilly pastel dress. The woman

Bella had seen with Grace the first day stood stirring something at the stove.

The moment the child saw her father, she dropped the cutter and tried to wriggle down from the stool, her eyes apprehensive. 'I'll get a cloth. I'll clean it. Heather said I could play—'

'It's all right.' Luc crossed the floor and gently lifted his daughter down from the stool. He didn't try to detain her, and his touch held no trace of the anger the little girl seemed concerned about. 'Dinner will be soon, *piccola,* so maybe you'd better wash your hands now. You can finish cutting afterwards, if you like. It doesn't matter if flour gets on things.'

The little girl drew a deep breath and seemed to visibly try to relax. 'I'll get ready right now. I'll be very fast.'

'Good girl.' As his daughter hurried from the room, Luc drew a deep breath, and turned to introduce Bella and Maria to Heather.

Bella murmured the appropriate greeting while her thoughts stayed on that interaction between Luchino and his daughter. She had hoped to see something better than uncertainty in Grace.

Heather efficiently served the meal while Luc poured drinks. Apple juice for Bella, accompanied by a teasing look she couldn't quite ignore, though she wanted to. The meal was delicious. A clear vegetable soup to begin, then prosciutto-and-ricotta-stuffed chicken breast wrapped in filo pastry and baked to perfection, served with salad greens and Roma tomatoes sliced longways and sprinkled with shredded fresh Parmesan cheese and paprika.

Luc worked hard to draw Maria out, sharing small anecdotes that brought Bella to laughter and warmed her towards him despite her resolution to remain aloof.

But Maria, although she did her best to appear relaxed, remained on edge and in the general 'good cheer' Luc's daughter remained quiet at his side, too.

When Luc offered dessert, small meringues filled with a tangy lemon sauce and topped with sliced caramelised banana, Maria shook her head. 'I-It's been a wonderful evening, but I—I'm afraid I've developed the most awful headache.'

'I'll take you home.' Bella got to her feet, as did Luc.

'I could drive both of you.' Luc, too, watched Maria with concern. 'Was it something I did, Zia? I want you to be comfortable with me.'

'No, no. You're a wonderful boy and I never thought I'd have—' She stopped abruptly, and her hand went to her temple. She looked as if she wanted to burst into tears, but maybe it was the pain of the headache? 'I should have contacted you when you first arrived in Melbourne. I'm so sorry I didn't do that. It was weak of me to avoid…'

'It doesn't matter. I don't mind.' Luc hastened to reassure her, but more pain washed across the lined face, and this time Bella felt certain it was emotional, not only physical.

'Say you'll see us again. That's all I need to hear.' Luc said it gently, but his gaze implored Maria.

'I want to be part of your life.' The words seemed wrenched from her. Maria then turned to Bella, clasped her hand and offered an apologetic look. 'It's been so wonderful to see… Luchino and my—and *Grace,* but I…I really need to go now. A taxi, if you please…'

'I understand.' Bella didn't understand at all, but if Maria needed the isolation of a cab ride home, Bella would give it to her.

'I'll phone for the taxi.' Luc excused himself to attend to it.

When he left the room, Maria's gaze followed him before she turned tortured eyes back to Bella. 'So many secrets,' the older woman murmured. 'It's too late…'

'What do you mean?' Bella took a step towards Maria. 'I don't understand.' If Maria could articulate her concerns, maybe Bella could help her. *Confide in me, Maria. Help me to understand this torture you seem to feel.*

Luc returned to the room too soon. 'A taxi should be here within minutes. They had one already in the area. Maria, can I get you some paracetamol in the meantime?'

'Yes, please.' Maria's voice quavered as Luc moved into the kitchen to get the tablets. Her face was now closed and cautious, and Bella knew any hope of drawing Maria out was gone.

The next few minutes passed in a kind of stilted small talk between Bella and Luc as they both hovered over Maria. Grace returned to the kitchen with Heather. The sound of the taxi's horn outside came almost as a relief.

Maria quickly turned to Luc and thanked him for the evening. 'Please forgive me for leaving. I'm just—it's too—'

'There's nothing to forgive. I only hope you feel better soon. I want this to be the first of many occasions, Zia. Hopefully future ones will end better for you.'

'You're an understanding man.' For some reason, this statement brought a hint of tears to Maria's eyes before she turned quickly away.

Luc walked the older woman to the taxi, and handed her gently in while Bella stood at his side and watched Maria and worried for her.

'I didn't like to send her away like that.' Luc led the way back into the house, and headed for the kitchen. He sighed. 'Let me get these desserts and we can have them in the lounge with coffee.'

'I'm not really hungry.' With Maria gone, Bella began to realise again the danger of being alone with Luc when she couldn't seem to convince her body to stop wanting him.

It would be better if she left immediately, yet when she saw that the nanny and Luc's daughter were absent from the kitchen she couldn't help but speak up. 'What can have happened in Maria's past to make her so uneasy in the presence of one of her family so many years later?'

'I don't know. There were whispers sometimes that I heard when I was small.' Luc, too, appeared deeply concerned by Maria's nervous state. 'I didn't understand much, but I gather there was a situation with a man. An engagement that went awry, maybe. She left the country suddenly.'

'And never went back.' It occurred to Bella that Luc could investigate that, too, but somehow she knew he wouldn't step over such a line. Why she had faith in that, she couldn't have said, but something in his expression made her certain of it.

'It was a different world then.' Luc paused. 'If she refused an arranged marriage or something, the family might have disowned her.'

'Maybe seeing you has raised unpleasant memories. If so, surely she'll get over that with time.' Bella paused, but there was one thing more she had to say. 'The pressure over her finances can't be helping Maria. If you told her the truth, she would know she doesn't have to worry about money.'

'If I told her the truth, she would realise she is indebted to me and feel even more pressured.' He shook his head. 'She's already too on edge to cope with that kind of revelation.'

Although she didn't want to admit it, Bella knew Luc was right. 'I suppose it will have to wait awhile, then.'

From upstairs, Bella could hear the faint sounds of splashing. A bath for the little girl, perhaps, then bed?

And Bella needed to go home to her bed, and not take thoughts of Luchino with her. A return to business matters would be a good idea, and she had just the way to do it. 'This afternoon I took on two commissions, both from ladies who attended that dinner ball. One of them also bought a pre-made gown.'

As she relayed the information, a little swell of pleasure

rose up and a smile twitched at the edges of her lips. 'We've sold five others to regular clientele, and a group of five women from the Yarra cruise have made an appointment to see me tomorrow to view gowns, too.'

'That's good. I'm pleased to hear it, cara mia.' He stepped towards her and somehow she couldn't get her feet to move to take her away from him.

Was he going to kiss her? Their gazes locked together and a part of her wanted it, but Bella found the resolve from somewhere, shook her head and stepped away from him.

Her legs weren't quite steady as she moved out of the kitchen and towards the front door of the house, but she tried to play it casual so he wouldn't know how deeply he affected her, with just the possibility of a kiss! 'I must go. It's late and I still have to drive home.'

'Actually, it's still quite early.' He pointed this out as he let his gaze rove over her. Clearly he didn't intend to let her pretend the awareness away.

Footfalls sounded on the staircase. Almost with relief, Bella glanced towards the sound, and there was Grace in her nightgown, cheeks rosy from her bath and bearing enough of Luc's stamp of likeness that Bella's heart squeezed yet again.

Grace hesitated, and then hurried down the rest of the stairs to quickly throw her arms around her father's legs. The embrace ended almost before it happened.

But Luc clasped the small back with his large hands, and seemed reluctant to release her as she stepped back.

He smiled into his daughter's eyes. 'Time for bed? Shall I read you a story before you go to sleep?'

'If you won't mind very much.' Quiet anticipation shone in the girl's eyes, making it clear this was a treasured routine in the Montichelli household.

'A story sounds like a lovely idea.' Bella tried for a light, farewell kind of tone. It was good, wasn't it, that Luc read to his child at night? A loving parent would do that, wouldn't they?

Not that her mother or father had read to her or her sisters, but their lives hadn't exactly been joyful, even before the parents had felt the need to terminate relations altogether. Bella drew a breath against the burn of unpleasant remembrance. 'And I'm going now, so your father will be able to come up very quickly to read for you, Grace.'

Bella would go home, be proud she hadn't yielded to kissing Luc. She didn't know what to say to Soph and Chrissy about Grace.

The little girl stepped past her father and cast a glance up at Bella. 'You don't have to go. You could stay for my story.'

Her gaze moved to her father. 'You like Bella a lot, don't you, Papa? If you like her, maybe she could be my new *mamma*, since my other one didn't want to keep me.'

The revelation came without any warning.

Now silence clanged all around them, clashed with the shock of the child's words. Bella heard again Lareen's voice on the plane five years ago, her saying that he'd fought for custody of the child, then left her with a nanny and ignored her.

Yet this was what Luc had told his daughter? That her mother didn't want her? Had the mother even been given a chance to be part of her child's life? Maybe not, and Bella should have thought of that before now. Just because she hadn't liked that one glimpse of Natalie, didn't mean the woman was as horrid as she had appeared in that short meeting.

Maybe she was pining even now for her daughter, while her daughter clearly pined for her! Bella turned an accusing gaze Luc's way. 'Her *mother* left her?'

She bit any further words down, wouldn't harm the child by discussing this in front of her. But oh, those questions fumed inside her and she would have her answers.

But Luc…didn't seem to notice her. Instead, his gaze was locked on his daughter and he swallowed hard. '*I* want to keep you, Grace.' He reached for his daughter and lifted her into his arms. Grace's little body leaned into his chest as though she needed his nearness. He kissed the crown of her hair. 'I told you that old nanny in Italy shouldn't have spoken about your *mamma* that way to you. And I'll always want you, for ever and ever.'

Grace dropped her head forward. 'Yes, Papa.'

'And we can get along fine without a mamma.' If anything, his tone was softer still. 'You'll start school here early next year. You'll be really busy then.'

Grace nodded again, then wriggled free of her father's hold. She stepped forward, until she stood quite close to Bella. 'You don't have to be my mamma. Did you have a meringue? I got to have one before my bath.'

Bella let out a tense breath and tried to go with the change of subject. The little girl probably felt uncomfortable for blurting her request, and Bella didn't want her to feel that way any longer than necessary. 'Sometimes I eat meringues, but I didn't have one tonight. My sister Chrissy would like the meringues, I think. She's expecting a baby and always seems to want things with lemon in them.'

Grace seemed to consider Bella's words for a long moment, and then she turned to Luc and spoke quickly in Italian.

Luc looked pleased. As some of the tension drained from his face, Bella admitted he didn't look like an uncaring monster. Oh, she didn't know what to think!

'I will do that, Grace,' Luc said, 'but ask me in English next time, please, if we're not alone.'

'My father will give you meringues. If you don't want them for yourself, your sister might like them.' Grace waited with her arms tucked against her sides until Luc moved towards the kitchen.

He didn't seem to want to go. 'I'll be back in a moment.'

As Luc walked away, a part of Bella wished she could walk away, too. She forced a smile for the little girl. 'It's generous of you to give me a gift.'

Grace nodded, but the moment Luc was safely away her body stiffened and she blurted as though she just couldn't keep it in, 'My nanny in Milan said my *mamma* was very beautiful and wore lovely gowns. You're beautiful. You wear lovely gowns.'

'My dear…I'm sorry.' Bella's arms wanted to hold Grace, this child with the shadows hidden in her dark eyes who longed so much for a mother. She clenched her hands at her sides as a wave of longing engulfed her, because a warning came right along with it.

This was not one of her lost sisters. This child belonged to Luchino, not to Bella, whether or not he was fit to be her father. And Bella…wasn't sure she could go to that place of caring and agonising all over again.

Grace's small mouth trembled as she spoke again. 'My *mamma* left me when I was a baby. I belonged to my father after that, but he left, too. I stayed with a nanny and when he visited I could tell I made him unhappy. He's only keeping me because I ran away. One day, he'll go away again.'

'He—he won't. He won't do that to you, Grace.' But Bella's whole body stiffened as a chill washed over her. 'How—how old were you when you ran away?'

Grace shrugged. 'I think I was five and eleventy-seven, but I'm a big girl now. I'm six.'

The confession almost made Bella smile, but the desire to do so quickly faded. If Grace had been five, then she was only recently united with her father, and that seemed to fit with the child's uncertainty around Luchino.

'Perhaps you should go up to your bed now.' Bella's hand

shook as she tucked a strand of gossamer dark hair behind the little girl's ear. She shouldn't have touched her. She knew it the moment her hand made contact, but it was too late, and her heart ached. Oh, dear God, it ached so much.

'You two look very solemn. What have you been talking about?' Luc stood in a casual pose, but his eyes were narrowed as though he sensed the tense atmosphere. He had a plastic container in one hand.

Grace cast a beseeching look in Bella's direction, and Bella spoke quickly, to allay the child's fears.

'We talked about…meringues.' They had, briefly. Bella told herself that was near enough, in the circumstances.

Luc's dark head bent to the child's and he rested his fingers on her small shoulder. 'The meringues are very yummy, indeed. Now run upstairs and hop in bed. I'll be there in a minute to read you your story.'

Grace ran halfway up the stairs, and stopped. From her position on the staircase, she pointed to the container Luc held. 'I hope you put in plenty.' Then she turned on those small bare feet, and ran the rest of the way.

Bella turned to Luc. Her heart began to pound as she prepared to confront him, and she worked hard to choose her words carefully even as the anger of years welled up. 'I didn't invite it, Luchino, but your daughter chose to confide in me when you went into the kitchen.'

'What did she say?' He seemed to brace as he waited for her answer. His eyes were remote. Not flat and lifeless, but guarded.

'Grace told me you'd left her with a nanny, and that she ran away to try to make you happy, as seeing her appeared to do the opposite.'

He looked as though she'd struck an arrow through his heart, but Bella couldn't let herself get caught up in what he might be feeling. Instead she saw the years of memories and hurt she and Chrissy and Soph had endured.

Luchino had put his daughter through that same pain, and Grace was so young, so defenceless. 'You wrested that poor baby from her mother's arms, then abandoned her for virtually years at a time, and only reclaimed her when she ran away. And you've convinced her that her mother didn't want her!'

Luc's mouth tightened to a harsh line. Dark pain passed across his face before a mask came down. 'Grace's mother *didn't* want her. Grace never should have learned that truth, but the nanny who had her back in Italy told her.'

'And the rest?' Bella could hardly speak the question, so great was the churning inside her.

His gaze darkened, narrowed. 'Why the sudden social conscience, Arabella? You weren't troubled by such a thing in Milan when you walked straight from my side, and into the show manager's bed. You decided he was a better deal, a better means of getting ahead in your career, so you left the poor "Diamond family" fool and moved right along.'

'What are you talking about?' Colour leached from her face. Nobody knew about that horrible encounter in the show manager's hotel room. But the expression on Luc's face said he knew, and had jumped to his own conclusions!

'I saw you leave his room that night, dishevelled, your face flushed and your hair all over the place. It was quite obvious what had gone on.'

What had happened was a fight to save her innocence, and it incensed Bella that Luc could believe such a horrid thing of her. 'The show manager lured me to his room with an invitation to a party. I wouldn't have gone, but I was upset and didn't want to be alone with my thoughts. I believed all the models would be there.'

Luc hesitated. 'What are you saying?'

'You heard me already.' Bella had no way to convince him, and she shouldn't have to convince him of anything.

'Then why did you look that way?' Perhaps he read the answer in her eyes, because his hands clenched at his sides and some of the colour receded from his face. 'He tried to harm you? *Dio.*'

'Yes.' She hated to discuss it. 'I got away, but not without… a struggle.'

Luc seemed lost, stunned. 'I'm sorry.' He muttered the words. 'This changes all I thought of you that night.'

Yes. It explained why he'd thought so poorly of her when he discovered her involvement with his aunt, too, but his apology was hardly a consolation to Bella now. 'I guess now I know exactly what you've thought of me all this time, maybe I should return the favour.' She stopped to draw a hard breath. 'I wondered if your daughter would have scars from your abandonment. Now I know the answer. What you've done is unforgivable. If I thought I had reason to dislike you before…'

'Grace is my business.' He took a step towards her. His tone was low and full of warning. 'Mine, Arabella, not yours. You may have shaken me with your revelation, but—'

'And how long will you keep her this time before you get sick of her and leave her again?' Bella's thoughts were all with the child, her emotions tangled in her own past, Grace's past and present, Luchino's distrust of her then, and still now.

It all meshed inside her in a big, bubbling mass until she simply flung words out, her voice shaking with distress. 'There are government departments in place to ensure the safety and security of children. DOCS, Family and Community Services.' Those places could help Grace where Bella could do little or nothing.

And they would let you back away so you didn't have to care any more about the little girl.

That wasn't the point!

'I would stop, if I were you.' Luc's head came up. Fury shone through the tight mask of his face. 'I would stop right now.'

But Bella couldn't stop. She held her ground, head up, emotions churning. 'Your daughter ran away because you made her so unhappy. Do you deny that?'

'She's safe with me now.' But he didn't deny anything, and a part of Bella wanted him to.

She wanted him to explain and somehow make this all better. Was it the child in her, crying out for reassurance because *her* parents had walked away? 'Grace is deeply unhappy…'

'Yes, and I made her that way.' Temper sparked in Luc's dark eyes. He stopped her movement towards the door with simply the power of his expression. 'But know this: I love my child, I will not hurt her again, and I would annihilate any person who tried to take my daughter from me. Is that clear to you, Arabella? You don't want to fight with me over this, believe me.'

His determination and care blazed from his eyes. But how could Bella equate that love with Luc's past actions that showed everything *but* love?

Confused, angry and threatened beyond anything she had felt since her parents left, Bella turned away. 'If you mean that, you need to talk to your daughter and help her to believe you won't leave her again.'

'And you, Arabella? What will you believe of me?' He tossed it at her as though he didn't care, but the glitter in his eyes contradicted that impression.

Bella drew a deep breath. 'If you can love your child, then I'm glad of it, and I know I have to conduct business at your side until I sell enough gowns to convince you to leave me alone.

'But beyond that I don't want to think of you, consider you, or in any other way be even aware of you.'

That was what Bella felt.

CHAPTER SIX

'YOU'RE troubled.' Chrissy made the observation to Bella in an undertone as they emerged from Luchino's office at the jewellery store and made their way back towards the store itself. 'You hide things so well sometimes, but I *know* you. I could feel the anger radiating from you, but also your *unhappiness*. Has something happened? Because I could still get Nate to buy you out of all this. He'd do it for you, Bella, no questions asked.'

'And have me hanging off his financial coat-tails for years?' A part of Bella wanted to say yes and just end it. But she couldn't ask that kind of financial investment of her brother-in-law. In any case, pride demanded that she not back down, that she resolve the situation for herself. 'Thanks for the thought, but I have to stick this out.'

'You don't, you know.' Chrissy gave a soft, sad smile as she contradicted her. 'It's not our parents deserting us. You don't have to prove anything or protect anyone but yourself. And you can resolve your situation by whatever means you choose.'

'I never regretted anything.' A fierce declaration from the depths of her heart. They didn't often talk about it, but Bella wanted her sister to know that. 'You and Soph saved *me*. Without my sisters—' She had to stop and swallow hard.

Chrissy's eyes grew misty until she blinked and determinedly squared her shoulders. 'Then tell me what's happened. Soph's been concerned about you, but she said you're not talking about it.'

'I had an altercation with Luchino.' Had it only been days since that happened? She and Luc hadn't seen each other between then and now, but each moment of that harsh encounter played over and over through her head. 'At one point, I pretty much…threatened to take his situation to a child-protection authority, and I found out—' she lowered her voice '—he thought I'd slept with the show manager that night.'

'He's hurting Grace?' Chrissy asked it in a whisper, but dragon fire flamed in the backs of her eyes. 'And he dared think such a thing of you?'

'He's not harming Grace physically.' Bella remembered her own anger at Luc. But she'd had time to think since then, to stop and consider his efforts to care for Grace. Intervention from a government authority at this point might be the most harmful choice of all for the little girl. 'But Grace believes he intends to abandon her again, that it's only a matter of time. As for that last night in Milan, I think my news shook him.'

Chrissy glared. 'He deserved to be shaken!' She paused. 'Will he leave his daughter again?'

'I—I don't know.' Bella's heart said Luc wouldn't leave Grace again, but her head said why not? He'd left the child before. Which was correct? Were either of them right? 'I'm so confused right now, Christianna, I just don't know.'

Chrissy linked her arm through Bella's and pressed their shoulders together in a show of solidarity. 'You're not alone. Soph and Nate and I are all here. If he does anything to upset you—'

'Soph will pound him to death with a hairbrush?' A reluctant smile came. 'That scenario has almost been played out once already. But I'm glad you're all here.'

When Luc decided to host this afternoon, a *Designs by Bella* and *Designs by Luc* occasion, by invitation only, Bella had simply invited her family along and informed Luc that the sisters all dressed in her gowns would triple the impact. Was she a coward for surrounding herself with her family?

'Soph's gone ahead to inspect the crowd in the store, and Nate's still in the office with Luc.' Chrissy fingered the soft folds of her gown. 'I guess maybe we should go out into the store, too.'

'Might as well. The sooner this is over, the better.' Bella touched a hand to the strands of diamonds and pearls that lay against her neck. 'I hope this is all fastened on securely, because I really don't want to lose any of it.'

Chrissy touched the jewels at her neck, too, and gave a reluctant laugh. 'I thought Nate was going to explode when Luchino tried to get me to exchange my necklace for this choker.'

'He calmed down when Luc explained it would help the success of the event.' The click of a door catch behind them warned that the men were about to appear.

Chrissy gave Bella a direct look. 'Just remember, we're all here. We're the three sisters, right? All for one and all that jazz. We stick together.'

'Like the grains of rice in one of Sophia's risottos.' Bella smiled despite herself, but the smile faded as the men came up behind them.

How could Luc have deserted his daughter? Didn't he know what that could do to her? Soph still felt so angry at their parents, and Chrissy had only recently admitted she had thought their parents left because of *her!*

Bella's feelings were torn in two. The one thing she knew was she needed to preserve an emotional distance from Luchino until they could be rid of each other.

Chrissy's husband slipped an arm around his wife's waist and bent his head to nuzzle behind her ear.

Luchino's gaze met Bella's and his expression revisited their last meeting. '*Bella.*'

They couldn't talk about it here, now. She didn't want to talk about it again at all. She pasted on a determined smile and gestured to the front of the store. 'It must be time to go mingle and impress the crowd with Montichelli jewellery and *Design by Bella* gowns.'

Anything to escape the thick tension between them. She moved towards the sounds of muted talk and laughter, towards the safety of numbers and of losing herself in the crowd. 'The more people we get to make purchases because of today, the better.'

'Yes, it's time, but we'll go in together.' Luc laid his fingers on her arm to guide her forward.

Just that, but her skin tingled and she felt so aware of his presence at her side. Bella resented that so much because she wanted to feel very *unaware* of him. She turned to glare at him.

'We need to present a united front to our guests, Arabella.' He guided her over to the throng of people in the store.

When he glanced at her, Bella read the frustration in his eyes and chose to see it as frustration at her.

'I'd started to trust you a little until I heard her pain from your daughter's own lips.' The low words forced their way out, and she realised they were true. But his actions were unforgivable. To treat them any other way was to trivialise Grace's hurts, and those experienced by Bella and her sisters, too. 'Now I never will.'

'Why is it such an issue to you, Arabella? She's not your child. Plenty of women…wouldn't even care.' Luc made a harsh sound in his throat.

'And I'm at the top of the list of women who wouldn't care because all I think of is money and me, and how I can bring the two together?' Bella had thought of money. She'd thought of ways to make sure she and her sisters had enough to survive! She didn't need to do that any more, but she remembered.

'I know I misread your behaviour in Milan that last night.' Luc let her see the regret in his eyes for only a moment before he masked it. 'But the way you used Maria is still proof of your...avaricious nature.' With an irritated growl, he gestured to the group nearest them. 'I intend to make you do the right thing by my aunt now, and that's really all that counts. So, let the show begin. Shall we, my dear?'

'Anything to speed the process of parting ways with you.' After that, Bella made the necessary social noises, all of it from some part of her not entirely connected to the rest.

As time passed, her gaze roved the store, involuntarily searched for a small face framed in dark hair.

'Looking for an escape route, Bella?' Luc dropped the words, soft and silky, beside her ear as they came together again at the edge of a group of people.

'Hardly that.' She wanted to draw away from him, but couldn't in the crowded area. A part of her accepted their closeness, too, even welcomed it, and she hated that. 'I haven't run from any of it. I'm doing my part.'

Bella pressed forward to join the next group of people. She insinuated herself among them with an overbright smile and announced what a privilege it was to match her gowns with Luchino Montichelli's original jewellery creations.

He would have no excuse to say she hadn't played her part this day.

After that, Luc left her to her own devices and she should have felt happy, yet somehow the afternoon seemed endless.

Chrissy eventually approached and let her know that she,

Nate and Soph planned to leave. She nudged her shoulder against Bella's again. 'Soph's got an appointment to do something with our landlady's hair. If it's radical, God save us all, but Nate and I could stay longer if you like. It's just that we said we'd drop Soph back to the apartment, and my back is aching a little from standing up this long.'

'No. Thank you, but I'll be fine. This will be over quite soon, and then I can leave as well.' Bella hugged her sister, then Soph as she approached. Both sisters were now *sans* their jewellery. Somehow Luc had slipped away to lock the pieces up and Bella hadn't noticed.

Even that irked her, which was really ridiculous, but she had been so busy avoiding him, and some of that time he hadn't even been in the showroom.

She pinned a bright look to her face and wished them well. 'Go home and put your feet up, Chrissy. I appreciate that you all participated in this with me. It meant a lot to know you were here to support me.'

As her sisters left, so did quite a few of the guests. Only a few people remained, and Luc stood chatting with several men who Bella suspected were placing orders for jewellery for their wives or significant others.

Bella noticed immediately when Grace and her nanny stepped into the store. The little girl stood very erect, her small face solemn as her gaze sought her father. Once she located him, her gaze moved to where Bella stood to the left, and her small face lit up. She moved to Bella's side.

'I thought we might be too late to see you.' Grace's gaze travelled over Bella's sparkling silver gown, the hair piled high on her head, the stunning diamonds and pearls at neck, ears and wrists. 'Oh, I wish I looked like you.' She sighed with longing, and it was such an ordinary little-girl thing to do that Bella was smiling back before she even realised it.

In a small flurry, the rest of the guests left. Luc locked the doors behind them, and Bella suddenly felt trapped, too.

'Let me return my jewellery, and I'll be on my way.' She moved towards Luc. She wanted him to take the pieces so she could leave.

'I thought we might celebrate the success of the afternoon and go for an early dinner.' Luc's gaze dropped to his daughter's face. 'What about *Papa's Piazza*?' His gaze moved on to the nanny. 'I don't know if you've been there. It's not actually an open square. It's a pizza place with a garden out the back. We could sit out there and Grace could make use of the play equipment.'

A family outing of a sort, Luc putting himself out to do something his daughter would enjoy. Bella began to remove the pieces of jewellery. If necessary, she would hand them to Luc right here because she *had to leave now.*

'Will Bella come with us?' A small hand reached out to touch the fabric of Bella's gown.

Bella tried to keep her tone relaxed, as though complex feelings weren't churning through her. 'I'm sure your father didn't mean to include me.'

I'm sure I don't want *to be included.*

Luc's expression darkened. 'You've worked hard this afternoon to help sell not only your gowns, but my jewellery as well. I'd like to thank you with a meal, even if a simple one. And if it would please my daughter to have you there...'

Bella had praised his designs because they were worthy of it. 'No thanks are necessary...'

'It's a lovely idea, Mr Luc, but I wonder if I could be excused.' Heather twisted her hands together. 'I know I'm not due for time off until tomorrow, but my sister's a bit unwell—an ear-infection that is resisting treatment. I'd like to pop across town and visit her, if that's all right with you.'

'Of course.' Luc agreed without hesitation.

Bella wanted to believe he did it to punish her, but she had a feeling he would have agreed in any case.

'If Heather doesn't come, what happens to me?' Grace searched her father's face with a worried look, but her hand slipped into his as though she expected to find comfort there.

'If Heather doesn't come, that just means your *papa* will look after you, the same as on Heather's days off.' Luc's words were calm and even as he raised the small fingers to his lips and offered a silly, smacking kiss that made the child giggle her uncertainty away.

'I'll be very good, Papa.' She seemed to want very much to please him.

'Even if you were very bad, Grace, I would still love you and want you with me.' Luc's promise to his child caught at Bella's heart.

It wasn't fair. How could he say such things, mean them, when he had left his daughter alone for so long? She opened her mouth to excuse herself, but from the corner of her eye, caught Grace's vulnerable expression.

And some of Bella's anger turned inward on herself, because didn't she want the child to be happy? If Grace wanted Bella to eat pizza with them, would it kill her to do that? 'I'll come. It'll be nice. I haven't had pizza for ages, except one Soph tried to cook a while back that seemed mostly to be made up of pine nuts and anchovy paste.'

Half an hour later they sat in the back garden of the pizza restaurant, Luc, Bella and his daughter. Just like a little family of three, Bella thought, if a rather well-dressed one with her in her very formal evening gown, and Luc in his tuxedo and starched white shirt. Oh, and the fact that she and Luc were as far apart from the idea of 'family' as it was possible to be.

Papa himself visited their table, exclaimed over Luc's

daughter, and assured them they were welcome. 'I suggest the garlic cob loaf first with jugs of juice and water and then—' he glanced at their faces '—one each of the house-favourite pizzas, white wine, and more juice for *la bambina,* yes?'

'Will you like garlic bread and pizza, Grace?' Luc addressed the question to his daughter, who sat at his side, her wide eyes taking everything in. 'You can have something else, if you want. Fettuccini, lasagne, minestrone soup...'

'Pizza, please, *il mio papa.*' She leaned towards him and whispered, 'I *know* I'll like it.'

Luc wrapped one large hand around Grace's small shoulder. 'Pizza it is, then.'

Maybe it was the influence of another Italian close by— Papa had greeted Grace in their native language and she had shyly enjoyed greeting him back. Whatever the reason, Grace had said those words. Even Bella, who couldn't speak Italian, could assume they meant something like '*my* Papa', which must have touched Luc's heart.

Was the little girl softening towards her father, learning to trust him little by little? If so, would Luc stand up to that trust, and would Grace ever be able to forget the past? Was Bella's own attitude changing, being lulled by Luc's apparent kind behaviour to the child and his acceptance of the truth about Bella's last night in Milan? If so, she needed to watch out for herself!

And his behaviour towards his daughter now didn't obliterate the past, either.

Luc watched Bella across the expanse of the small table and wondered why he'd forced her to be here tonight. She didn't exactly look happy right now, and he could guess he was probably the reason for that. But a glance to Bella's left gave Luc the answer.

Grace had slipped into the chair beside Bella partway through the night. Now she lay asleep against Bella's side.

Bella's free hand stroked absently over Grace's dark hair. For his daughter, Luc would do anything.

'Your sister must be close to her due date to deliver the baby.' It was a ploy to distract himself from his thoughts, but in fact Luc *had* wondered how Bella's pregnant sister would look in one of Bella's designs. He needn't have worried. Bella made magic with her gowns and Chrissy had looked wonderful.

The sight of her pregnancy had brought memories to Luc that inevitably led to thoughts of Grace now. His daughter and his guilt were his companions. He loved the one, and accepted the other. He doubted Bella had any inkling of any of that.

Uncertainty flashed across Bella's face before she smoothed her expression. 'Chrissy's due in a bit over a month. Hopefully the baby won't be too big or anything.'

Why the unease? Luc wondered, but then she cleared her throat and glanced guiltily at the child pressed against her side.

'She won't rouse.' Grace slept like Luc's brother, Dominic, heavy and deep. Luc pushed the thought away. 'I'm sure your sister's delivery will be trouble-free.'

Luc remembered another delivery, the joy and awe that had inspired him that day. So much unhappiness had followed, but on that day he had felt humbled and challenged and determined to love his family, to be a good father, a good husband. In all of it he had tried, and failed.

'Are you happy about your sister's pregnancy?' He watched her face, but she only lowered her gaze.

A short shrug, a nonchalant look. 'It's a wonderful thing for Chrissy. I've been sewing baby clothes for months.'

Her words didn't explain the unease and uncertainty she probably believed well-hidden from him.

I've had experience with unhappiness, Arabella.

But maybe she was simply concerned for her sister's health and well-being.

He quietly got to his feet. 'You did well today at the store. And thank you for joining us for dinner. Grace enjoyed your company. Please convey my thanks to your sisters, too, for wearing the gowns and jewellery with such style and finesse this afternoon.'

Bella rose, too. 'They both enjoyed the chance to dress up, and to wear your jewellery.'

'We should head to our cars.' He lifted his daughter up, a limp burden in his arms. When he reached the cars he settled Grace into his, and turned back to Bella.

'You wouldn't even know there was a child in there.' She gestured towards the dark interior.

No, and for a long time there had been no child in his life, no happiness, no closeness of any kind.

Loneliness brushed against Luc, surprised him with its sharp ache. He wanted to pull Bella into his arms and somehow find solace in her from that empty feeling. His thoughts towards her had changed and he didn't know what to do about that.

Bella had still misused Maria. That hadn't changed, so why this tilt in attitude towards her? Yes, he had jumped to conclusions about her past behaviour, but... 'If Grace moved, you'd see it. In stillness, the tinted windows mask what's inside.'

'Like you.' Bella threw the words down, and turned away. 'You mask things, too.'

'Do I?' Luc grasped her wrist, but released her almost immediately, burned by that single touch and by the need to have so much more from her than a touch. Burned by his conflicting feelings about Arabella. 'I can see you want to say something. Why the silence? Is it because you don't believe I'll care for my daughter now and you're trying to work out what to do about it? I warned you—'

A fierce well of emotion rose in him. 'If that's on your

mind, you can let it go. Grace is *mine,* and I will never leave her again.'

'Grace grew up with a nanny watching over her until she became so unhappy, she ran away.' Bella fired off the words with hurt in her tone, although she kept that tone lowered. 'How do you expect me to respond to that, Luchino?'

She thrust her chin forward in an aggressive movement. Thrust one hip forward, too, and her fists balled at her sides. 'Obviously for a long time you *didn't* want her enough to keep her with you.'

'You don't know…' In fact, the opposite had been the case. Grace's mother had used her as a bargaining chip, to get more money out of him and finally as a weapon to hurt Luc, but he couldn't admit the truth without exposing things about Grace that he had promised himself he would never reveal.

'I know you left her. What else matters?' Bella trembled with leashed feeling. 'You left her just like my parents left me, Chrissy and Sophia. Left her high and dry and didn't care less about her.'

'I can only tell you again that I care about her now.' Luc couldn't explain more to Bella.

But this—Bella's revelation—revealed so much that he hadn't understood. 'You said your parents were travelling and you didn't see them. I thought you mightn't have got along or something, but you're judging me by their actions, aren't you?' And Bella had been hurt. Something deep inside him ached at that thought, softened towards her despite himself.

'I'm judging you by your own actions.' Bella gave a harsh laugh, gave him no quarter. 'I can never accept that you chose to leave your own child. Maybe you *will* look after Grace properly now. Maybe she will grow to trust you and even get over the past eventually, but *I* don't trust you. I never will.'

CHAPTER SEVEN

A WEEK passed. Bella's tension didn't ease at all. When she climbed onto a plane that would take her from Melbourne to Sydney for a major fashion event with Luchino, she didn't know how she would cope with his nearness. At least sales were up in the store, and they received more enquiries every day. She and Luc had attended three more events, but they had barely managed an uneasy truce.

That truce was uncomfortable, in part, because she still couldn't shake off her awareness of him. Each time they were together it only seemed to plague her more. She saw it in his eyes, too, and that didn't help her to stay strong against him. Bella clenched her fists in her lap and wished she were some place else. Anywhere.

'Does air travel bother you?' Luc glanced at her hands. 'Statistically, flying is still a very safe way to travel.'

Even now, he sounded concerned, *nice,* and how could she see him that way?

'Getting on a plane doesn't concern me.' No more than it should, anyway. It was getting on the plane with Luc at her side that was the problem.

Since that night at *Papa's Piazza,* Bella had turned herself inside out emotionally in an effort to come to terms with Luc's past behaviour and his behaviour now. The one conclusion she had finally accepted was that Luc loved his child and wouldn't leave her again. He was just too fierce in his determination for Bella to believe he could be swayed from his decision.

It would be so much better if she could simply stay angry at him anyway, but it wasn't that simple any more because she saw good alongside the ruthlessness. He was showing it now. Her hands left her lap, and tightened on the arm-rests of her seat. 'I don't like to leave Melbourne, that's all.'

This was true, although it really shouldn't matter much these days if she decided to travel now and then. 'Not that my sisters need me underfoot all the time. They're perfectly independent, just as they should be.'

A pain jabbed at her heart as she said the words, and Bella suppressed a frustrated groan. It was *good* that her sisters no longer needed her so much. They had grown up, grown into themselves. She was *happy* about it!

'Leaving Grace was harder than I imagined it would be.' Luc's face tightened momentarily. 'We haven't been apart since...before we moved to Australia.'

Since his daughter had run away and he reconciled with her?

'I told Grace I would be back before she even goes to bed tomorrow night.' His lips pursed. 'In the end, I think it will do her good to know that I can leave and come back as promised.' He hesitated. 'I hope so, anyway.'

'At least it's only overnight.' She said it as much for her own comfort as his.

If they were in Sydney for a single night and most of that night was taken up with work, surely she would be able to keep her thoughts away from, well, from this awareness of him.

The plane taxied along the runway. Luc's hand came to rest over hers just as the aircraft lifted off and started its swift climb into the sky. Bella's heart did a swift climb, too, and it wasn't only because of the burst of engine power driving the plane, or the change in altitude.

He's simply holding your hand. Get over it! Better still, put a stop to it. She moved her hand out from beneath his, and immediately felt the loss, which wasn't how she wanted to react. What was happening to her?

A recorded bell sound came over the plane's speakers, and the captain introduced himself and assured them they were in for a great flight.

'I wonder if they ever say anything else.' The random thought, any thought, was better than dwelling on Luc's effect on her. She sat up straighter, determined to remind them both of the purpose, the *only* purpose, of this trip. 'We're here on business. That's all we're here for.'

'Is that an attempt to warn me off wanting you, Arabella?' The calm words, spoken in his mellow accent, shivered over her skin. The expression in his eyes was anything but calm. 'Because lately I find that I…do.'

She held her head up high and refused to shift her gaze from his, even though she felt exposed. 'If it's necessary to warn you, then yes, I'm warning you off. You don't trust me. I don't trust you, either. It's best to stick to business and hope we can survive that much.'

'And will you warn yourself not to want me, too?' He didn't wait for her to do more than gasp her outrage before he moved on to a completely different topic. 'You've made a good choice with your models.' His lips twitched upward. 'They're doing a great job of getting your gowns out there.'

First he exposed the fact that he knew she was attracted to him, admitted he wanted her, too, and then he praised her work efforts. Bella's reactions couldn't keep up, but he *didn't* trust her, so it must be a shallow kind of desire he felt for her!

Determined to seem unaffected, she returned a small smile

of her own. 'A few Montichelli jewels scattered here and there don't hurt, either.'

She could talk about work, keep this focused in the way it should be focused. And the gowns and jewellery *had* made quite a splash at Luc's store extravaganza that day. Now they had a wonderful invitation to model both together again at a top Sydney fashion show, hence this trip.

'Have you considered hiring a seamstress, now that you have more work to cope with? Maria mentioned you've got a number of commissions to get through, plus alterations to pre-made gowns.' As he made the comment, Luc's gaze roved over her face.

Warmth followed his glance. He almost could have touched her, she responded so clearly to just his look. Bella drew a slow, deep breath and willed her skin not to reveal its sudden heat to Luc's piercing gaze. 'Actually, I've just hired someone to help with some of the sewing; a friend of a friend who works in costume design at a local theatre. She's willing to be paid on commission.'

'Good. It's important you don't over-extend yourself.'

'I thought you might oppose the financial investment.' In fact, she had expected he might be angry that she hadn't consulted with him about this. 'It's taking away from Maria's overall profit margin.'

'I want your cooperation, but I don't want you to drive yourself into the ground with too much work.' He shifted his gaze to the window, but not before Bella caught the look of something akin to weariness in his eyes.

Was he as confused by all of this as she was? By the way they seemed to drive each other crazy yet still respond to just being close?

Unwilling to think about it, Bella snatched at the first thing that came to mind. 'Maria seems more highly strung with each day that goes by. I'm worried about that. She looks forward to her visits with you and Grace so much, talks about them in advance and can't say enough about both of you afterwards. With more money coming in, I thought she would worry less, yet she seems almost brittle with anxiety at times.'

'I enjoy seeing her, too. She's very good with Grace.' Luc absently adjusted the small ventilation knob above him, and dropped his hand to the chair's arm-rest once again. His arm was so close that Bella could shift slightly and brush it.

She tucked her elbows against her sides and sat very still.

'Through my finance manager, I've done everything I can to reassure Maria on a business level.' Luc's brows drew together. 'Until she relaxes with me personally, I don't know what else I can do. Sometimes she seems quite comfortable, happy, and then she seems uptight all over again. I asked her once if she wanted to tell me what was bothering her. She came close to bursting into tears and I promised I would never ask again.'

'I've almost asked, too, but if she doesn't want to confide her worries, we have to respect her privacy.' Bella sighed. Lately she was just as nervy as Maria! She wished for the flight to be over so she could at least not be seated almost on top of Luc in the small, confining chairs. He was too close, too masculine, too attractive and tempting and…

'An allowance in my favour, Arabella?' Luc accompanied the question with a teasing glance that made her insides quiver. 'I'm shocked. I wonder what will be next.'

Not kisses, even if those were what filled Bella's imagination at this moment. She would get over this, get her brain back from outer space and focus only on her models, on what they had to achieve with this trip.

The whole reason she and Luc were together was because Luc believed she had ridden roughshod over his aunt, pushed her into an unfair agreement. *Ergo,* because Luc *didn't trust Bella!*

And his past behaviour towards his daughter should make it quite clear that Bella must not trust him.

'What's next is making a success of this fashion show.' She turned her air vent on full force and aimed it right into her eyes. Maybe a continuous blast of air, even aeroplane air, would somehow help, because Bella was struggling to focus, and that was not a good thing!

All evening at the modelling event, Bella avoided Luc. At least, as much as she could as she saw each model safely onto the catwalk, gowned and bejewelled and determined to dazzle the masses into purchasing Bella's creations—and maybe a few Montichelli jewels, too. Avoidance seemed a smart idea.

When they treated the girls to a meal after the show Bella did her best to focus her attention on her models, rather than on Luc. It wasn't easy with him so near, and her senses re-acting to him so strongly.

Luc in full charm mode wasn't easy to ignore either, yet he didn't flirt with the others. He simply made them feel good about themselves.

And they sighed over him, the Italian single-father who hauled out his wallet and proudly displayed his daughter's photo after he'd excused himself to phone home and check that everything was OK with Grace. Luc passed the photo around then tucked it back into its slot in his wallet, stroked his finger over Grace's image. Bella's heart caught, too. She couldn't help it.

Dinner finally ended, the models went to check out a casino nearby that purported to have good live music.

And Luc and Bella were alone.

'The show was a success.' Luc's low-spoken words washed over her as they walked the quiet, empty hotel corridor towards her room. Déjà vu walked with them because they had shared a hotel six years ago, too. Luc had walked her to her room, taken her in his arms and whispered how much she had come to mean to him.

'There's something *you* should know about that last night in Milan, Bella.' Luc stopped before her door, pushed his hands into the pockets of his dress trousers. His jacket fell back, revealing the whiteness of his shirt, the beautiful sculpting of his hard chest and flat stomach. 'I hadn't intended to tell you, I felt the time for that had passed, but now that I know you weren't seeing the show manager…and I'm attracted to you—'

He seemed to hesitate, then admitted, 'I wasn't being unfaithful to Natalie. We were already separated.' One of his hands lifted to cup her face, and she couldn't move away.

Nor could she think clearly! 'What are you saying? You'd had a baby. Grace could only have been a few months old.'

'Natalie and I…married for the wrong reasons.' He held her gaze, the liquid brown of his eyes calling to her senses, even as she tried to absorb his words. 'The marriage was shaky throughout the pregnancy. By the time Grace arrived it was on the rocks, and Natalie's total uninterest in the baby once she was born, and the fights we had over that, put the final nails in it.'

'Why didn't you tell me this at the time?' What if he had really cared for Bella at that time? What if he hadn't simply been toying with her? Her perceptions rocked on their foundations. 'Why tell me now?'

Luc's muscles rippled beneath the shirt as he drew a deep breath and let it out again. 'I was too caught up in wanting you. Everything else faded away.' Heat from his palm warmed her skin as he stroked her cheek. His fingers flexed against her chin. '*Dio*, Arabella, I wanted you then, but I want you more now. I want you to give yourself to me.'

The hotel hallway was dim and silent. Bella's anger and

unease were also quiet, silenced perhaps by the shock of Luc's revelation. How could she think of past hurts when her body, her senses could only think of him? Of this? Of right now? Yet she sensed a warning in here somewhere, if she could only focus on it.

'Have you missed it, Bella? This? Us?' Luc stepped forward, clasped her shoulders in his hands.

She shivered. Every pore of her skin felt his touch. 'Yes, but I'm not sure…'

'Don't think. Just feel. Respond to this, to us.' The steely muscles beneath the cloth of his jacket flexed beneath her fingertips when he encouraged her touch. She wanted to touch his bare skin. Luc had been separated that night. His marriage had already ended, if not in the paperwork.

Why *shouldn't* she respond to this? Other reasons escaped in the heat of her awareness and need.

'We're not those people any more. We're only this, now.' His words brushed over her.

They *weren't* those same people, yet…

He murmured her name, lowered his head to brush the lightest of kisses across her lips and Bella lost the battle with her thoughts. She wanted him to hold her, and everything else faded away.

When he laid his mouth over hers, plundered, swept her up against his body, she acknowledged every line and angle pressed against her softer form, the possession of his lips, and it felt so good.

'Luchino.'

'Not Luchino. *Luc.*' He nipped her earlobe. Buried his head in the crook of her neck and inhaled.

Shivers rushed down her spine all the way to her toes. And she said it. '*Luc.*'

'Yes.' Luc's mouth returned to hers and he took her with

his lips and the press of his body and the soft murmur of mellow words each time their mouths parted so they could draw breath.

And Bella lost herself in that soft, sensuous journey. In Luc.

'Where's your key?' The question breathed into her ear as his hands roved up and down her arms, across her shoulders. 'I want to kiss you in privacy.'

Her body responded in instant agreement. Deep in her mind a small warning registered, but Bella was not capable of heeding it. Not right now. Her bag had dropped to the floor. She retrieved it and a moment later Luc had her room key in his hands.

It seemed important that she be the one to do this, so she took the key card, swiped it and opened the door.

Luc followed her in. One lamp burned beside the coffee-table in the sitting area. Before she could consider turning any other lights on, Luc pulled her back into his arms. They were right inside the door and he pressed her back against it, his mouth on hers before she could distil a single thought.

In Milan they had shared kisses, had walked arm in arm as he escorted her to her room, but he had always walked away. Now she realised he might have done that out of respect to both her and his still legally married state. Again, the basis of her thoughts towards him shook, and seemed to support exploring this.

'You taste good, *mia Bella,* better than the best wine.' As if to prove it, his tongue traced the seam of her lips. He tasted so good, too, and her lips opened on a sigh.

He pulled her tighter against him, kissed her deeper and harder until her senses reeled and her heart pounded as a wave of longing washed over her. And she admitted, 'I want this more than I could ever want wine.'

'Then let us taste it together.' He responded to her words

with an onslaught of touch, with deep, drugging kisses and whispered words of praise as his hands moved over her. 'Your waist is so tiny. I can span it with my hands.' He proved it, and the feel of his fingers spread across her soft flesh, even with cloth between, made her shiver.

'I want to…touch you, too.' She was caught up in sensation as she pushed his jacket down his arms and off, then ran her hands over his chest and shoulders. 'We never did this.' Never touched this way, so intimately.

'No. I wanted to.' His hands skimmed upward from her waist, over the sides of her ribcage. He drew her hard against his chest and she felt the combined beat of their hearts. Fingers closed gently over the mound of her breast and his mouth came down hungrily on hers, capturing her gasp of pleasure, her welcoming response.

Somehow his shirt was gone, too, and Bella traced the muscles of his shoulders, his upper arms, explored the hot wall of his chest with the tips of her fingers until he crushed her to him. His body shook as each angle and plane pressed to her softer contours and the fire of need burned hotter, stronger.

'You trust me now.' He must, to reach out to her this way. He must have realised she didn't intend Maria any harm, wasn't money-hungry.

Luc didn't seem to hear her. Instead, his hands sought and found the small hidden zip at the side of her dress. Tugged.

Maybe it was the brush of cool air against her sensitised flesh that finally made Bella think. Really think for the first time since he'd started to kiss her. Or maybe it was that Luc hadn't responded to her words.

Did she draw a breath? Stiffen? She didn't know, but his fingers stilled at her side. Dark glittering eyes searched hers while desire stamped its signature high on his cheekbones and in the sensual, hungry line of his mouth.

'I want you, Arabella. I want to see all of you, touch all of you...'

But the fog of hunger and awareness fell away, and Bella saw what they were doing, had almost done and most of all she guessed that he *didn't* trust her. And worse, she didn't trust him, and she had forgotten that. She pushed away from him, set her clothing to rights and wrapped her arms around herself. 'You want me sexually, but you don't believe in me. If you did, we wouldn't be together, working to make my gowns sell because you believe I owe it to Maria to recoup every cent of her investment to make up for coercing her *into it.*'

'This isn't about that.' But he didn't deny it. Instead, he rammed a hand through his hair. It was already dishevelled from the touch of her fingers. He still looked too gorgeous for her peace. 'I wasn't exactly thinking just now—'

'Neither was I.' Bella had thought with her senses, had allowed her desire for him to push aside other issues and lead her to this.

'Don't bother to say anything else.' She didn't want to hear another word. 'What you think of me doesn't matter because I know who I am and how I behave. I'm more concerned that I forgot what *I* know of *you*. It's more than what I believed that last night in Milan, or what you believed of me. I'm glad for my conscience's sake that you were separated at that time, but this is about what you did to your daughter, your belief that I'd misuse your aunt financially, the way you forced my compliance in business. It's about all of those things.'

While she spoke, he had replaced his shirt and shrugged the jacket back on. 'You can say all those things, but this was also about you and me and what we wanted tonight. I still want you. Maybe that's something we both need to think about, because you were there with me, Bella. You shared every moment. You wanted me as much as I wanted you.'

She had. That was part of what bothered Bella so much, but if he didn't believe in her and she couldn't trust him, what was left? Nothing worth having!

Luc didn't wait for a reply. He moved to the door, opened it and stepped through. Only then did he turn to look back at her. 'Think about it, Arabella.'

And then he was gone.

CHAPTER EIGHT

BELLA went to bed with her mind in turmoil. It stayed that way as she fought memories of Luc's kiss, his touch. Those moments together hadn't meant the same to him as they had to her. He didn't respect her.

So make him believe in you.

But why should she try to do that? Luc was distrustful of her and a man who had left his child high and dry. He must have had a reason, yet what reason could be good enough? There was none.

And why should Bella grovel for him to believe in her?

Your arrangement with Maria was *loaded your way.*

That was true, but she had believed Maria to be easily able to carry the burden until the money started to roll in for her. It was an *omission* on her part. Nothing more.

With a muffled groan, Bella buried her nose in the pillow and prayed for the oblivion of sleep.

Eventually she must have drifted off. The ringing of her cellphone woke her when it was still dark in the room. She answered it with her eyes half-closed and her heart beating hard. Was it Luc?

In her sleep-fuddled state it didn't occur to her that he would simply phone the room, or knock on the door. 'Yes?'

'Bella, it's Soph.' The tension in her sister's tone banished thoughts of Luc and brought Bella swiftly upright in the bed as Soph went on. 'Chrissy's at the hospital. She's had some bleeding, contractions, and they're worried about the baby.'

'Oh, dear God.' Bella scrambled from the bed and started to fling things into her overnight bag. Her legs felt like jelly and her hands trembled.

She had to get back to Melbourne, to get to Chrissy. 'I'll get the earliest flight I can. Are you at the hospital with her now? What exactly is happening? Can I talk to her? Where's Nate? Which hospital did he take her to? What doctor is looking after her?'

Anxiety made her questions sharp, and when Soph began to answer, she cut her off. 'Actually, there's no time for that now. I'll call you from the airport once I've secured a flight. You are with her, right?'

'I'm at the hospital, but they haven't let me in to see her and I had to come outside to make this call.' Soph took a quick breath. 'I'll come out again every half hour and check for a message from you. That's the best I can do. You just have to come back, that's all.' Her youngest sister hung up on her.

Bella felt helpless. For one long, overwhelming moment she acknowledged that she was here and Chrissy was back home in Melbourne and it could be hours before she got to her, and even when she did Bella couldn't make things better for her. That work rested in the hands of the hospital staff, and they had better do a stellar job of it!

'Nate will look after Chrissy. He'll see she gets the best care, and I'll get to her quickly. I'll make it happen somehow.' She said it out loud to try to reassure herself, but couldn't help but remember the strain in Soph's tone. Why wasn't Soph with Chrissy and Nate? Was their sister in isolation, in an intensive-care unit?

By the time Bella had dressed and slung everything together, her nerves were stretched until even the tendons in her neck stood out. A sharp rap sounded on her door. She whipped it open ready to give whoever stood on the other side a quick dismissal.

Luc waited there, his face beard-shadowed, his bag in his hand and concern in his eyes. He looked disreputable and desirable and far too kind and concerned for Bella's peace of mind. Heat prickled at the backs of her eyes and she blinked hard.

She wanted to walk into his arms and be…comforted, to forget last night and all the unease between them. It was a far too emotional way to feel towards him, yet she saw no harshness towards her in his expression, only care.

'Sophia called my room.' He said it as though this were the most natural thing in the world. 'I've phoned ahead to the airport and got us on the next flight. It'll be tight, but if we move we'll make it. Let's go.'

'I'm ready. I was about to leave when you knocked.' *I didn't need you to rescue me.*

Why had Soph called Luc? Had she forgotten Bella always handled her own challenges, and for a time she had handled much of her sisters' for them, as well?

Now Luc just took over, hustled her into the lift, out of the hotel and into a waiting taxi cab. He barked the destination at the cab driver in a tone that said 'hurry', and told him there'd be a hundred dollars in it if he could shave ten minutes off their drive time.

'I could have managed this for myself.' Bella made the comment as the driver took the incentive to heart, and they were slammed back against the seat as he roared off.

Luc raised an eyebrow in silent question and Bella again admitted he looked appealing in his day's growth of beard. She, on the other hand, didn't have a skerrick of make-up on and would no doubt have puffiness under her eyes from lack of sleep.

Ah, she shouldn't waste time worrying about a few smudges under her eyes at a time like this.

'Sophia seemed to think I might be able to help smooth the path for you.' Luc offered the words in a calm, matter-of-fact tone, but his eyes revealed awareness of last night, and confusion for a moment before he looked away.

Maybe he didn't want to think about it.

Bella didn't want to, either. Not now. Maybe not ever.

And those stressful feelings that had built over previous months raged through her now. Chrissy needed her and she would be there for her. Her sisters would always have all of her heart and commitment, but Bella now accepted she couldn't go through loving any one else in the way she loved them. The years and their parents' abandonment had taken their toll on her, and she had finally realised that.

When the taxi screeched to a stop in a no-stopping area in front of the airport, Luc handed the man the fare and tip. 'Thanks. We've got the bags.' He leapt from the cab.

Bella had a flash of Luc inside her room last night, his arms around her as he pressed her close, so close, as though he couldn't bear for them to be apart. Why remember that now when it was just her imagination and all he had wanted was sex and she had appeared willing? And then there wasn't time to think of anything as they sprinted from check-in to their departure gate with their small bags clutched in one of Luc's capable hands.

On board the plane, Luc stowed their bags in the overhead-locker space and settled beside her. His broad shoulders seemed to form a protective barrier between her and the rest of the passengers. 'I guess your exercise routine includes some jogging? You handled that sprint very well.'

Small talk was good. She would take what distraction she could get if it helped her not to think about last night, and not to dwell on her sister's predicament. 'I don't have a routine, really, but I like exercise. I do Pilates, yoga, running; whatever works at the time. It makes me feel good. Other calming influences include *chai* tea and being anywhere that Sophia isn't when she's cooking or experimenting with hair.'

Luc gave a muted crack of laughter that somehow lightened her stress, even if just for a moment. When the plane began to taxi along the runway, his smile faded and he lifted her chilled hand into his. 'I'll get you to Chrissy's side as fast as I can, Arabella. I know you're worried.'

Something in that caring tone, despite the unease between them, despite last night's interlude and the knowledge that it must never be repeated if she wanted to hold on to her sanity, loosened Bella's tongue and words poured out. 'Do you have any idea how many things can go wrong with a pregnancy? What if she loses the baby? She'll be devastated. She's building a family with Nate. Chrissy needs that. I *want* that for her. She must be able to have that.'

'You love her a lot, don't you.' It wasn't a question, but an observation.

She nodded and fell silent, and didn't want to admit that his hand over hers helped her to keep herself together.

When they arrived in Melbourne, Luc guided her the fastest way through the crowded terminal, then circumvented the taxi queue with an ease that made Bella blink.

As she climbed into the cab, she tried to regain control of the situation. 'I can take things from here.'

Distance. That was what she needed. Lots and lots of distance between her and Luchino Montichelli, in any of his guises, so that she could remind herself of all the reasons she really wanted nothing to do with him. 'I'm sure you'll want to get home to your daughter.'

'Grace isn't expecting me for ages, and I don't intend to leave you until you're sure your sister will be OK.' Luc climbed into the rear of the taxi beside her and gave the driver their directions.

A muscle twitched in Luc's jaw. He pointed to her handbag where it lay on the floor. 'Why not ring Sophia? If she can talk to you now, she might be able to alleviate some concern. At the very least she'll know you're almost there.'

'Yes. I'll ring Soph. That's…what I was just thinking, too.' Bella grabbed her phone. Luc was thinking for her when she should have thought for herself. Next thing she would *expect* him to help her! 'Soph may not be outside the hospital, but I'll try.'

Sophia didn't answer the call, but the phone rang in Bella's hand a few minutes later. Bella jumped. She felt Luc's gaze on her, but when she glanced towards him he had turned to look out of the window. 'Soph?'

The conversation wasn't long. To Luc's credit, he simply sent an enquiring look her way when it ended. Bella shrugged. 'Soph still hasn't been allowed in to see Chrissy. Her phone battery is almost dead. She said she'll meet us at the hospital entrance and explain things then.'

Bella realised she had included Luc in her comment. Her mouth tightened. 'You don't have to stay. As I said, I can manage perfectly well without you.'

She didn't *want* him to stay. Between last night and this morning, Luc had witnessed more than enough vulnerability from her already, thanks very much. As well as portraying himself in far too good a light today for her peace of mind.

To help that peace of mind, Bella gave her credit card to the driver, agreed on a cost plus tip, and watched him process the payment at the next set of lights. She would have to repay Luc for the other out-of-pocket expenses later.

Luc sighed. 'I'm staying, Bella. Stop wasting your energy on this.'

The hospital came into sight and Luc's gaze scanned the buildings. He helped her out of the cab, grabbed their bags in one hand. Luc's other hand wrapped around her elbow and she just didn't have the willpower to shrug off that surprisingly comforting hold.

Besides, they were hurrying towards Soph, so there really wasn't any time to do much about it in any case.

Sure, Arabella. You go on believing you did anything but soak up his touch because you wanted it.

Did not!

When they drew level with Soph, Bella's youngest sister started to speak, her words raspy with concern and emotion. Bella hugged her, and then listened while Soph poured out her fears and frustrations.

'They said only one person could be with Chrissy because her blood pressure went crazy, so it had to be Nate.' Soph fought to pull herself together. 'He's emerged twice to tell me Chrissy said not to worry, but he's worried himself. She's had contractions and it all started with some spotting. That can't be good.'

At this confirmation of Chrissy's problems, Bella's own blood pressure hiked to match anything her pregnant sister might be suffering. The Valkyrie cry of battle roared through her and she turned to face the entry doors of the hospital. 'They don't understand. We will see our sister, *right now,* because she needs us and will feel better for it.'

Pity anyone who got in the way of Bella making that happen.

But Luc had already pushed through the doors and stood talking to someone at the admissions desk. He appeared to be charming them. Bella's eyes narrowed as she fought the sudden deflated feeling and a sense of helplessness because even this purpose had been taken from her.

'Come with me.' Bella grabbed Soph by the arm and hurried up to Luc.

He turned and clasped her free arm and poured some more charm onto the woman behind the desk. Phrases like 'family need to be together' and 'perhaps the patient could be asked if she'd feel better with a short visit from her sisters' poured from his tongue in a tone and accent guaranteed to curl the sturdiest, most sensible of toes.

They curled Bella's toes, enough that it took long moments for her to find the words to tell Luc to butt out. By then, the woman was halfway to eating out of his hand. Then Luc poured the accent on even thicker, and *begged* for the girls to be allowed to see their sister—for Chrissy's own sake.

Bella couldn't believe it, but strings were pulled, because they were outside Chrissy's room minutes later. Bearing Luc's behaviour in mind, Bella turned to glare at him and…what? Berate him for making happen what she had needed to happen? For making *her* want to fall at his feet with that performance?

No. For wresting control from her when she needed it to keep herself together. What did she have left, except her control? Everything else felt so uncertain, she wasn't even sure who she was and what she wanted any more. The thought was more terrifying than anything she could remember, because purpose had kept her going.

Luc met her confused stare with a steady one of his own. He shoved his hands into his pockets and half turned away. 'I'll wait while you find out how your sister is doing.'

Now irrationally, perversely, Bella wanted him to insist he go into that room with her, that he face whatever lay on the other side, *right at her side*.

She blinked, narrowed her gaze and floundered once, then

twice, for words to thank him for his misguided efforts, to dismiss him, to assert herself somehow and regain the feeling of control that she so desperately needed now. Any of the above would do.

'Come on.' Soph tugged at her arm.

'Go inside, Bella. I'll be here.' Luc turned away, left her in the clutches of her youngest sister.

Bella put everything from her mind except Chrissy and her unborn child, and with Soph trembling at her side she stepped into Chrissy's hospital room.

'How are you? How's the baby?' Bella clasped her sister's hand and let her gaze rove over Chrissy's pinched features and the tummy bump beneath the bedclothes. 'How do you feel?'

Chrissy returned Bella's grip with a firm one of her own. 'They've tested and checked me for every known complication on the planet, and have ruled out lots of nasties. The doctor's inclined to think the contractions and rise in blood pressure were brought on by panic when I saw the spotting, and my blood pressure's settled down since they admitted me.'

Good. That was all good. Bella nodded and spared a glance for her brother-in-law. Nate looked like hell. His fingers stroked up and down Chrissy's arm and over her tummy as though he couldn't bear to stop touching her and the baby.

The intimate picture brought a pain deep inside Bella. It was a good picture, a loving picture of a man and a woman who were meant for each other. This sister had found her soul mate, Bella realised. She hadn't fully understood that truth until now. But somehow the picture also made Bella feel a little lost.

Soph stood beside Bella. In a moment she would move so Soph, too, could assure herself first-hand that Chrissy was OK. There were other questions first. 'Have the contractions stopped, and what about the bleeding? What explanation have you received? Has that stopped, too?'

'The contractions have stopped.' Chrissy's relief showed through as she said so. 'And there were only a few spots and they've stopped now, too. It's not from a low-lying placenta or one that's detached from the wall of the uterus. Everything seems OK and they tell me up to thirty per cent of cases of spotting during pregnancy are never explained, so I shouldn't worry just because they didn't find a reason.'

Chrissy's hand came to rest on her tummy. 'The doctor says I'll just have to be careful, rest up. If it starts again at all I have to come straight back in.'

'They'll let her go home tomorrow morning, if her blood pressure stays down and everything else is still OK.' Nate lifted his gaze to meet first Soph's, then Bella's eyes. His hand clasped Chrissy's over the bump of the baby. 'I'm sorry you weren't allowed in until now and that you've both been worried.'

Chrissy gave Nate an affectionate tap on his arm. 'Not that *you* were worried. You only calmed down a few minutes ago when the nurse took my blood pressure again and it looked so much better.' Then she sobered and turned to look at Bella and Soph again. 'I admit I was worried, too. Thank you both for being here. I didn't mean to cut your trip short, though, Bella.'

'Don't give it a thought. I wanted to be here.' Bella clasped Chrissy's hand one last time. She wanted to stay longer, but knew if she tried it, a nurse would soon be along to throw them out anyway, and that might upset Chrissy again.

Also, Chrissy needed to rest now that she knew they were all nearby. Bella should leave without a fuss and, after all, Nate would stay on. 'See you do rest, Christianna. You're in good hands here. Nate will make sure you do all the right things. We'll *all* take care of you until the baby arrives. Whatever it takes, you can consider it done.'

'I know.' Chrissy dashed at a tear that trickled down her face. 'I'm all hormonal or something at the moment.'

'You wanted your husband and you wanted your sisters. That's perfectly normal.' Bella hugged Chrissy and felt it when her sister relaxed. She let go and stepped back as she fought to control her own relieved emotions. 'Why don't you visit with Soph for a quick minute and then we'd best leave you with Nate again?'

She turned to the man in question. 'You will let us know immediately if there are any further problems? We'll see Chrissy again tonight and then tomorrow, whether she's at home or still here. More often if she needs us, but we don't want to get in the way of her resting—'

'I'll keep you informed.' Nate nodded. Then he rounded the bed and pulled Bella into a quick hug. 'I'll take care of her. I promise.'

'Thank—thank you.' Bella cleared her throat to get rid of the sudden tightness there, and turned to Soph. 'I saw the car as we arrived. I need to say a few words to Luc, and then I'll meet you at the car when you've said goodbye to Chrissy and we'll drive home, OK?'

When Bella stepped out of the hospital room, her gaze caught Luc's. He saw that her eyes were overbright, and tension radiated off her.

She dropped her gaze. 'I wasn't sure you'd still be here.'

Luc pushed his hands into his pockets because he wanted to pull her into his arms and she didn't want his touch. She had made that clear at the end last night and was making it clear again now that she had seen her sister and had a chance to pull herself together.

He shouldn't want her, either. She wasn't for him, had used his aunt in business. *It was true* that Bella had negotiated a one-sided deal with Maria. But the woman who had rushed to her sister's side today and who responded in his arms so openly last night had a lot of care and compassion in her.

But now wasn't the time to pursue this. 'How is your sister? Will she be OK? Is the baby OK?'

'They should both be OK, provided Chrissy rests and takes proper care of herself and the baby.' The smile Bella cracked seemed relieved, if a little forced and a whole lot reluctant towards him.

'I'm glad to hear that.' He allowed his gaze to examine her strained features as he spoke and, again, wanted to comfort her. 'I'm really glad, Arabella.'

'Sophia will be out in a moment.' Bella moved over to the bags stacked against the wall. 'I said I'd meet her at our car.'

'I'll walk you there.' Luc took up both bags.

Bella glared at him and snatched her bag into her own hands. 'I can carry my own things. I can control what's happening to me...' She stopped, seemed to realise her outburst revealed far more about her than she might have wanted, and moderated her tone. 'It's good of you to want to help, but it's just a bag.'

'By all means, carry it yourself if it pleases you.' But this wasn't about just a bag, and Luc wondered why Bella needed that feeling of control so much. Because her parents had taken that from her when they left her in charge of her sisters?

They made their way in silence until Bella drew level with her elderly bug car.

'This is it.' She unlocked the vehicle and tossed her bag into the back seat, then turned to him with palpable reluctance.

Did she think he expected her to thank him for his help this morning? Luc's anger rose at the thought. He dumped his bag to the side and spoke before she could. 'I helped you because your sister asked me to, Arabella, and because I was there and I could. I know you could have done it all yourself, but there's nothing wrong with accepting help.'

'I appreciate that you wanted to help me.' Bella's words were clipped, her face tense as she stared at him. 'I *do* appreciate it, Luc.'

'Do you?' Warm sunshine shone down on them. Luc stepped closer, until his hands held her forearms. They stood face to face.

Bella tipped her head back and glared at him. In a moment, she would tell him to let go, and he would do it. But first, Luc looked down into her face that was so much more than a particular alignment of bone and flesh, of nose and mouth and coffee-coloured eyes. And he realised he wanted to understand her. He *needed* that.

'Tell me about your sisters. Tell me how it was without your parents.' His mouth tightened. 'I need to understand your anger. It's part of what's between us.'

'It won't help. It won't change anything.' Bella stepped away from him. He felt chilled without her presence, but eventually she spoke. 'I was eighteen when our parents left us. My sisters needed someone they could depend on. I had to be it.'

'Were you even out of school yourself?'

She nodded. 'I'd just finished and been scouted by a modelling agency who saw my photo in the paper with our school netball team. Christmas was getting close. It wasn't exactly a great present our parents gave me and my sisters that year.'

Luc wanted to take her pain away. He knew he couldn't. And this was why Bella blamed him so personally for leaving Grace.

You need to be blamed. What you did was wrong.

Luc knew that, too. He faced the guilt every day. He always would, but even so, he didn't want Bella to feel that way towards him.

Bella's mouth tightened and her gaze clouded. 'Chrissy and Soph always pulled their weight and did their share, but they were still schoolgirls. They couldn't carry the emotional weight. They weren't ready.'

'You did that for all of you.' It explained a lot about Bella, yet he sensed there was more. 'Your sisters are adults now, and run their own lives. How does it affect your life today?'

Even as he said it, he recalled that Chrissy had wanted her sisters at her side while concerned for her baby's security. She had a husband, but she still needed her sisters. Luc's heart ached because he had lost that sense of family. In fact, he had never really known that, despite living as part of what the world acknowledged as a family unit.

His parents had never seemed to really accept him. Dom had been the favourite. Maria seemed more willing to reach out to him than they had been, and Luc felt a different connection there, but Maria had her secrets, too.

So many tangled threads. Was it even possible to unravel them, let alone weave them into something good, something that would hold together in his life? What did he want? Of Maria? Of Arabella? Of his life?

'Chrissy and Soph are adults, but everything I have inside is still tied up in them.' Bella's gaze focused again, and revealed so much hurt. 'Sometimes I feel like the well has dried up, and I'm scared if they need me I won't be *able* to help them. I've been so empty, Luc, *so empty inside for so long.*'

'*Dio.*' He reached for her.

But Bella made a harsh sound in her throat, part laugh, part pain, as she backed from his touch. 'We were abandoned in an unforgivable act of selfishness and I've tried to compensate for that loss to my sisters every day since. You—you've put your child through the same pain. I forgot it for a while last night, and today I let you help me, but I *mustn't* forget. I won't let myself.'

Grace was younger, but she *had* suffered and, while Luc hoped one day Grace would fully let go of those bad memories and be able to simply be a happy, contented child, it was now clear to Luc that Bella didn't want to ever forgive Luc his actions.

If he had any thought of keeping Bella in his life in more than a business sense, he should give that thought up right now, because it would never work. His chest tightened as he faced the fact.

'I need you to only work with me to sell gowns from now on.' She stood in place, faced him, but somehow moved away more emotionally as she went on. 'Anything else can only hurt both of us.'

Her pain was in her voice, in the emotions that moved across her expressive face. Luc couldn't stand it. 'Arabella, my dear—'

'I— There's Sophia.' Palpable relief filled Bella's tone as she quickly turned away. 'I have to go. Goodbye.'

CHAPTER NINE

BELLA wasn't booked to attend another function with Luchino until Friday. Grateful, she buried herself in work at the store, in making sure Chrissy continued to look after herself and the baby, and in not thinking about Luchino. A great deal of time went into not thinking about Luchino.

On the Friday morning, Maria left Hannah in charge of the customers, took Bella outside into the wild, windy weather, hustled her into the nearby coffee shop, chose a corner table and with a great deal of agitated hand twisting confessed her financial situation. She concluded with, 'I've made a habit of overspending. I still have to go on buying trips but I intend to choose more judiciously in future. I want to bring things to rights.'

Although Maria didn't say it, Bella guessed she felt bad for allowing Bella to believe she was wealthy when they had cut their deal. But how could Bella remain angry at the older woman when she was clearly in such distress?

It wasn't Maria's fault that Luc blamed Bella for hammering out that five-year agreement.

And the agreement *had* been unreasonable. Bella just hadn't realised it at the time and Luc, by his actions since, had made it clear that only one course would be accepted as recompense. Bella was doing her best to cooperate in that respect, but she felt on a knife-edge emotionally.

'Thanks to the notice I've attracted while Luc and I have…gone about together, my gowns are selling well.' Bella made a deliberate attempt at reassurance. 'I'm sure things will turn themselves around.'

'I'm sure, too.' Marie stirred through the froth on the top of her cappuccino with a spoon. 'I have a silent backer. That has taken the strain off financially. The backer is a philanthropist and the agreement I signed with him is airtight and can't get me into trouble, but I felt you should know about this.'

She stopped and cleared her throat. 'I'd have brought it up sooner, but I've been rather on edge about…other things lately, and found it difficult to broach the subject.'

'Thank you for telling me.' Bella wished she could be equally open to Maria, tell her she already knew these facts, but it was Luc's job to discuss this with Maria.

Maria went back to the store only long enough to retrieve her suitcase, and then climbed into a taxi to head for the airport and the next buying trip in question. She should have looked less worried after her confession, but that aura of suppressed tension stayed with her.

With the wind at her back, Bella leaned into the cab to touch her employer's arm. 'Have a safe trip. If there's anything else I can do for you, or you want to talk—'

'It's family matters, Arabella, and what's done is done. I'm lucky to have this chance now…' Maria drew back and pressed her lips firmly together.

Bella forced back a sigh. A frown between her brows, she straightened. What chance was Maria referring to? The chance to have Luchino as family here when she had left her family so long ago? Yes, it must be that. But what exactly had driven Maria away in the first place?

Surely her boss would open up about it now, as she had done about her finances? 'Why did you leave, Maria? Why did you come all this way so long ago—?'

But Maria pulled the door closed from inside, probably didn't even hear. The cab drove away.

The afternoon didn't exactly get better. Bella sighed as she ushered the last customer out of the store and finally locked the door. *Maria's* had done a strong trade, especially for a Friday, but not all that trade had been positive.

Maybe it was the odd weather setting everyone off, but today she'd encountered not one but three very difficult customers. Two had tried to return goods they had clearly already worn. When Bella pointed out the 'no returns' sign over the cash register, well, it was fair to say the women in question weren't exactly agreeable.

After that, Hannah came down with an upset stomach and Bella had to send her home. Then, to cap it off, a woman who had made an order for a custom-design gown phoned to cancel it because she had changed her mind and wanted her deposit back.

Bella stood firm. The deposit would not be refunded, but she now had a half-made gown she may or may not be able to sell.

And tonight she had to see Luc again. Had to go out with him and schmooze more people to try to sell more gowns, until she reached the point where Luc would finally back out of her life and not take her places again, not see her again in that way. In a bid for some sort of control, Bella had insisted she obtain the tickets for tonight's theatre performance. It seemed silly now, but at the time it had felt important to her.

Now she had to phone Luc and tell him when and exactly where to meet her for their evening together, and her heart rate picked up at the thought of hearing his voice.

Just the thought of his voice!

Oh, she needed help.

'Hello, *Diamonds by Montichelli*, this is Kayla. How may I help you?'

'Ah, Kayla. Hi.' *Why have you answered Luc's private office line?* A well of something suspiciously green-coloured rose up in Bella's mind. 'Is Luchino about? It's Arabella Gable. I need to speak to him about our trip to the theatre tonight.'

There was a pause. One of those loaded ones that set imaginations off and running.

Bella did her best to suppress hers.

After a moment, Kayla cleared her throat and spoke. 'I thought someone would have let you know—Luc's housekeeper, or the hospital. There was an accident.' She drew a quick breath. 'One of the new light fittings came down. It almost hit a customer. Luc saved her, but it caught him on the head. The fittings are heavy…'

'Luc's been hurt? Where is he? How bad is the injury?' Bella's stomach knotted. Wind began to howl around the exterior of the store in earnest and push at the panes of glass as though determined to get inside. It fed the tension already on the rise inside her.

Naturally Luc's staff would believe he would let Bella know of his accident. They thought he and Bella were involved.

In the background behind Kayla, Bella heard someone ask for the woman's help. Kayla excused herself to speak briefly with the person.

She came back on the line and said rather breathlessly, 'I'm sorry. I'll have to go. A group of overseas tourists just swamped the place. It always seems to happen right on closing time. Luc went to the hospital, and then went home. That's all I know. I assume it can't be too bad if they let him out.'

'OK, thanks for your help.' Bella, too, now wanted to end the conversation. She hung up and attended to the last-minute stuff in the store while her brain wrestled with this new information. Luc had been hurt, taken to the hospital. She hadn't even known about it. How was he now? Was he truly OK?

Bella exited and secured the store, and walked the several city blocks towards Gertie's day-long parking bay. As she hurried along, she used her cellphone to ring Soph, explain the situation and offer her the theatre tickets.

'They're on the bedside table in my room, tucked under the clock.' She hadn't put them there so she could look at them before she went to sleep, anticipate another night out with Luc or anything silly like that. It was just a safe place to keep them. 'I have to go, Soph, and I'm sorry I've had more than my share of the car lately.'

'Don't give it a thought.' Soph paused. 'I might just put those tickets to good use, though. I'll do my hair and wear a wonderful dress and look sophisticated and glamorous.'

She stopped and cleared her throat. 'Take care, Bella. I've realised you care about him, but Luchino is still the one who hurt you…'

'Oh, but I don't…Luc and I aren't even—'

'Sorry. Joe's at the door to help me paint my nails. Gotta go. Thanks for the tickets.' Soph ended the call.

OK, so their friend and neighbour intended to let Soph talk him to death while he painted her nails. If Joe let himself in for that, it was his own fault. Bella squirmed a little with the thought that Soph had observed her interest in Luc, but there was no time to dwell on that now.

Bella had to find out the extent of Luc's injury. By the time she reached the car she was jogging, with the wind hard against her back. She climbed into the yellow bug and drove directly towards Luc's home, justifying all the way and telling herself this didn't mean she was overly worried, or too personally invested.

For example, if Luc might be out of commission for more than a day or two, Bella needed to know so she could plan her time around that. So what if they didn't have any other engagements organised after tonight for several days? That really wasn't the point. Did she even know the point any more?

'Bother the whole thing!' She drove Gertie right up under the protective portico at the front of Luc's house, and jumped out into an even fiercer wind. On Luc's porch, she pressed the doorbell and waited. And waited. She raised her hand to press the bell again, but someone finally answered.

'Oh, Arabella. I'm sorry, I know I should have contacted you but Mr Luc wouldn't have a bar of it when I suggested it.' Heather stood with her hand wrapped around the door handle. She looked more than a little overwrought as she stepped back and gestured to the interior of the home. 'Please, come in. You'll want to see him straight away, and I'm sure he'll feel better when he sees you.'

The housekeeper seemed more than distracted. She seemed really worked up.

Bella's heart dive-bombed into her shoes. 'Is—is he really bad?'

Heather didn't seem to be listening. 'I'll see if he's still awake. The man hasn't slept a wink since he got home, although I'm sure some rest would do him good.' Heather hurried up the staircase and disappeared.

'Heather. Oh, wait.' But it was too late to get cold feet now and what would she have said to the other woman, anyway? Bella wouldn't rest until she saw for herself that Luc was OK. To do that, she had to see him, face to face.

It didn't have to be a big deal unless she made it into one and if he was awake, he couldn't be almost dead, surely? Bella stood in the foyer and waited for the housekeeper to return. She longed for a pot of tea. Even a cup of the less than stellar *chai* hot-chocolate blend Soph got at the supermarket last time would do. Or maybe a very long run would get the tension out the best.

'My *papa* got whacked on the head, but he'll get better.' The announcement came from Bella's left.

'Grace! My goodness, you—ah—I'm sorry, I didn't notice you'd joined me.' Bella turned to look down at Luc's daughter. The child seemed calm enough. 'I know Luc got, ah, whacked on the head. I thought I'd check to see how he's feeling.'

'Well, it was right on his noggin.' The little girl sidled closer to Bella and knocked on her own, before she informed Bella in an educational tone, 'But Montichellis have tough noggins. That's why he'll be fine. He just has to stay in bed and be quiet until tomorrow. I readed to him out of one of my books to help him feel better, too, and it worked.'

'That was nice.' And the sparkle in Grace's eyes said she had enjoyed that closeness with her father. *Why did he desert you, Grace? I just don't understand.* Bella could no longer even try to reconcile those actions with the man she knew and…cared about?

Only a little. Only enough to want him to be all right! 'I'm glad you're not worried about your *papa*.' Bella wasn't quite willing to accept she had nothing to worry about until she saw him, though.

Heather returned down the stairs. Her almost beseeching look concerned Bella. 'Mr Luc will see you now. He's resting in his room. It's the third on the left at the top of the stairs.'

Again, Bella's nerves tightened. 'Is everything all right, Heather?'

With a glance at Grace, who seemed to have absorbed every word of the adult conversation so far, Heather hesitated, and then blurted, 'My sister rang. She's had a fall at her flat. It's that dratted middle-ear trouble. It's wreaked havoc with her balance for weeks. She says it's nothing and she's probably right.' She waved a hand. 'I'm sure she's fine. I can visit her tomorrow, once Luc is back on his feet again.'

Totally unacceptable.

Every sister-raising, protective, watch-over-her-loved-ones instinct in Bella rejected the thought that Heather should wait until tomorrow to check on her sibling. 'Could she get a taxi to take her to a hospital accident-and-emergency centre, just to get checked over?'

'She's too stubborn to go.' Again, Heather shrugged. 'Over the phone she does sound fine, just a bit annoyed, and she says she's a bit bruised from the fall itself.'

Bella said the only thing she could say. 'You must go to see her straight away, Heather. There's no reason I can't…take care of things here until you get back. Why don't you go right now? Just tell me what I need to do for Luc and Grace while you're away.'

Grace made a slight sound at Bella's side. 'Does this mean you'll be my nanny for tonight?' Her eyes lit up with unaffected anticipation. 'Will you get my dinner and read me a story and put me to bed?'

'Of—of course I will.' A fatalistic kind of acceptance swept over Bella. She couldn't avoid this and remain true to herself, she had to help out. She would cope somehow.

Bella smiled into the small, vulnerable face and saw her sisters' younger faces. Soph and Chrissy had turned into wonderful women, despite their parents' behaviour, despite any mistakes Bella might have made. Grace was so much younger. Maybe she *could* forget the past, particularly if her father continued to build love and security all around her.

Again, Bella's foundations teetered as she struggled with conflicting feelings, and with her own vulnerability.

Heather interrupted Bella's labouring thoughts with an

outline of what needed to be done to watch over Luc in the next few hours. She ended with, 'Hourly checks of his pupils and overall lucidity are the most important of it. They may not prove necessary, but it's better to be cautious.'

'Absolutely.' Bella listened as Heather explained that her sister lived on the other side of the city and estimated how much time it would take for her to get there, check on her sister and return.

Then Grace piped in with, 'I'll watch TV while Bella checks on Papa.'

Without further ado she turned into the comfortable living room, and raised the volume of a children's cable station. She glanced back out to where Bella hovered beside the nanny. 'I'm allowed to watch this channel.'

'OK.' Bella's lips twitched.

Grace was definitely happier, more confident, and it couldn't all be down to the nanny's influence, although Heather seemed a lovely woman. *Luc* had achieved this.

Bella tried not to notice the softening of barriers inside of her. 'You go on, Heather. I'll check on Luc, and then watch over Grace until you get back.'

A muffled bellow from upstairs made both women start.

Heather recovered first with a wry smile. 'I think that'll be Luc, wondering why you haven't appeared by now. He doesn't like the confinement, but the doctor said he has to rest until tomorrow.'

'Go. Take whatever time you need, to see to your sister's well-being.' Bella drew a breath. 'I can cope.' Yes, Bella could cope, but possibly not with the sight of a very sexy, very disgruntled man tucked into a sinful king-sized bed in a masculine room that smelled of his cologne.

'Hi.' She hovered inside the doorway, and cleared her throat in the hope she could produce a stronger tone of voice.

He didn't have a shirt on. She couldn't exactly miss the fact. Indeed, it was a warm day, warm enough that she felt comfortable in her flowing trousers and sleeveless blouse. But Luc…he should be covered from the chin down—for her own safety. 'Should you be sitting up like that?'

Pillows propped him up from behind, and his arms were folded across the luscious, sculpted, almost too perfect bare chest smattered in black hair that arrowed downward. A chest Bella had explored with her hands—

'My head feels the same whether I lie down or sit up. I have a bump on one spot, it's tender if I touch it and yes, I have a bit of a headache, but I could be up, doing things…'

He muttered something about over-zealous fresh-faced doctors who issued silly orders to confine a man who needed to work. 'I'm sorry about the theatre. I'll get tickets for something later in the week instead. I only remembered it when Heather said you were here.'

'I told Soph she can use tonight's tickets. Once you're better, we can think about going to another performance.' She ventured nearer to the bed. It wasn't rank stupidity on her part. She needed to see close up that he really was OK.

Luc had colour in his face, his eyes looked fine. She stared into them a little more until she realised her focused attention had resulted in an elevation in her pulse rate. A deep, interested growl of sound erupted from Luc's throat, and made her aware he, too, had reacted to her scrutiny.

'I just wanted to check you were OK.' She felt compelled to explain, to assure him, and herself, of her sane, sensible reasons for this visit. She didn't want him to think any *other* reasons came into it. 'As one colleague to another.'

'I guess that's why there's a heat haze coming off the walls in here.'

His growled words certainly raised her temperature!

Luc leaned back further against the pillows, and ran a hand through his already tousled hair. A lock of it flopped onto his brow in appealing, little-boy disarray.

Something inside her melted, even as heartache rose, because even without anything else she didn't have the capacity to cope with…loving him or wanting to form a family with him. Oh, dear God. She didn't…almost love him, did she?

No. That couldn't be possible. Feeling frantic, Bella turned her thoughts to practicalities, forced them there! 'Um, there's something you need to know.'

At her careful tone, his eyes narrowed. 'What is it?'

What if Luc didn't want Bella to watch over him and Grace? Maybe she should have consulted him before she let Heather go to see her sister. 'Ah, Heather's sister had a fall and Heather was concerned about her. I sort of told her I'd hold the fort here while she visited, made sure everything was OK, that kind of thing. I'm sure it won't be for too long—a couple of hours, maybe.'

'OK.' Again, he focused that narrow-eyed gaze on her and seemed to see right inside her thoughts.

'Just "OK"? You're not angry? You don't mind?'

'Mind having you in my home for the next few hours where I can look at you, know of your presence even if you're not in the room with me?' He gave a short bark of laughter. It ended fast enough that she suspected he might have made his head ache afresh. 'It might be sheer torture, but no, I don't mind.'

When he leaned back against his pillows Bella was sure his head pained him. She couldn't let herself think of his welcoming words with their sensual undertones.

'Let me help you get comfortable, and then I'd best go see how Grace is getting along.' It would be smart to get out of Luc's range, out of the danger zone. Because she was too close to him, and wanted to be closer still. 'I didn't come here to…make things difficult for either of us, Luc.' She wanted him to believe that. 'I guess—I just needed to see for myself that you were well, and then Heather had to go…'

She reached past him to ease all but one of the pillows from behind his back so he could lie flat. 'You should try to drowse a little. Surely your body wants that.'

The hot look he gave her indicated his body wanted *her.* 'I suppose I could try to rest while you give Grace some dinner.' His brows drew down. 'We usually rustle something up on Heather's days off, so Grace won't mind "easy" food. She likes cheese on toast, spaghetti Os, poached eggs…'

'I'll find something suitable, and I'll bring you something, too.' Did he think Bella didn't know how to feed one small girl? She had prepared meals for herself and her sisters many times throughout their lives, childhoods included. Their mother hadn't exactly embraced domestic activities.

As she grasped the pillows, Bella's fingers brushed the skin of Luc's back. Hot skin that made her stop very still, pillows gripped, knuckles against tempting flesh as she drew a sharp gasp of air and her senses whispered all sorts of beguiling ideas.

'Move the pillows, Arabella. Do it now.' He grated the words, but his tone held more than anger or pain, and all her senses reacted. Luc, too, inhaled sharply.

Bella's whole body now tingled with awareness of his. She shifted the pillows, gripped his shoulders to help ease him to a prone position. Leaned over him and it was too indicative of another kind of closeness.

Oh, heck. She shouldn't think about Luc prone in bed full stop. Her hands didn't want to let go. She forced them away from him, pretended a great interest as she smoothed the light covers over his chest, but that simply brought her too close to his skin again.

'Your injury.' She avoided eye contact as she hovered at the side of the bed. 'Can I get you anything while you wait for your dinner? Did they prescribe painkillers?'

'I don't need painkillers. Was it just altruistic concern that brought you here, Bella?' He asked it in a controlled tone. 'Because I'm getting a different vibe from you right now.'

'I phoned the store to check on travel arrangements for the trip to the theatre.' She hedged. 'Your employee had little choice but to tell me what had happened. I understand you were the hero of the piece and saved a customer when the light fixture crashed down.'

Maybe if they focused on that, Luc would forget to pursue the topic of the possible reasons behind her visit.

Luc's gaze dropped from hers. 'I just happened to be close by at the time.'

'I'll bet your daughter thinks you're a hero.' The teasing words slipped out, but Bella felt rather proud of him, too. Proud and possessive and...

A hint of pain touched his face before he smiled. 'I think I've made some progress with Grace. She's learning to trust me more, to accept when I say something I mean it and will stand by it.'

'That's—that's good.'

After a moment he allowed his eyelids to droop. 'I appreciate you arranging for Heather to leave to see her sister. If she'd told me, I would have stayed awake to watch Grace so she could go.'

Bella wanted to tell Luc to take care. She wanted it almost as much as she wanted to run her hands all over him. She opted for the safer choice, and pointed out his foolishness. 'You may think you have a very mild concussion. That's probably all you do have, but you can't know for sure. Hence the doctor's *thoroughly sensible* order that you rest in bed until tomorrow.'

On these words, Bella turned one last glance towards the tempting bed and nodded approval as Luc finally allowed his eyelids to close. 'Let yourself rest, Luc. I'll be back to check on you soon enough.'

CHAPTER TEN

'YOU always look really pretty.' The comment came from Grace as Bella put the children's book back on a shelf filled with wonderful little-girl stories, some of them narrated in Italian, some in English.

Grace's bedroom flowed over with treasures of the kind Bella would have chosen herself. Cuddly bears, dolls in a cradle, all sorts of fun and educational toys piled into a big box in the corner of the room. And books. Loads and loads of wonderful books that even a child of Grace's age could become lost in for hours.

Some of the toys were old and well-loved. But somehow Bella knew Luc had provided all of them for his daughter, even when he hadn't been with her.

Bella walked back to the bed and tucked the sheet around Grace's small shoulders. 'Thank you. I have to dress a certain way for my work, but when I'm at home I like to wear comfortable things. Most of the time I make them for myself, because I also find sewing…soothing.' She almost said cathartic, although she had little time to sew for herself these days.

Grace reached her arms up in clear invitation for a cuddle.

For a short moment, Bella's heart seemed to stop as all her

emotion welled to the surface. Care, concern, pleasure in the presence of this child who was *Luc's* child, not Bella's.

Bella took the hug, returned it, and noted Grace's eyelids drooping. Her heart ached with feelings she didn't want to think about, so she squeezed the little body once more and released her. 'Goodnight.'

She whispered the word against a baby-soft cheek, gave herself just one moment more to inhale the scent of little girl and soap, scents of innocence and youthfulness, before she turned away.

At the door, she flicked the light switch, and left the room.

Bella went downstairs. As she watched the news on the TV, the wind outside finally died down. The phone rang as the programme was ending. It was Heather, to say she couldn't get back because of flash-flooding on her side of town.

'I saw it on the news.' Bella's hand tightened around the phone. 'I'll stay until morning. Please don't even attempt to get back before daylight.'

Bella gathered her bag and went upstairs. She checked on Grace again. The child did indeed sleep heavily. Beside Grace's room, Bella discovered an empty bedroom that appeared to be in good order. She dropped her bag on the bed, left her shoes on the floor beside it and went in search of supplies. It was going to be a long night.

'No need to tiptoe. I'm not asleep.' Luc murmured the words as Bella hesitated in the doorway. The soft lighting of the hall cast her in silhouette so her golden hair shone like a rumpled halo around her head.

She'd apparently found the pile of clean clothes sitting folded in the laundry room and helped herself. His T-shirt reached to her mid-thighs. A swimsuit would reveal far more, but this was different. For all he knew she could be naked under there, and in any case, something about her wearing his clothing…excited him.

As if he needed any help in that department. 'You look like you're dressed for a long stay.'

'Heather is stuck on the other side of town. They had quite a storm over there.' She drew closer.

Luc couldn't let her lean over him and peer into his eyes again while he lay there passively. Instead, he shifted and sat up on the edge of the bed. 'I feel fine, Bella, better than good and able to…take on anything. But that's probably not something we should discuss in the middle of the night when you look like that.'

'Oh.' She tugged the hem of the T-shirt in sudden self-consciousness. The movement flatted the material across her breasts.

Small, rounded, perfectly formed breasts that Luc wanted to touch and caress until they were both mindless with desire for each other.

'I'll just check you out and leave.' Her lips pressed together and her gaze moved all around the room. Anywhere but directly on him, it seemed, but her cheeks had flooded with scorching colour. 'I mean, I'll check your state of health, and then I'll go to bed. In—in the spare room.'

If she said it outright, she couldn't have announced more loudly that she, too, had thought of sharing his bed, *this bed right here and now,* with him. Luc clicked the bedside light on. It bathed the room in a soft glow and only served to make her look even better to him.

He wanted his arms around her so much that they ached. But all he could do was clench his teeth and hope she didn't realise the strength of his hunger for her. 'Go ahead and check me over, but I'd suggest you sit down. I find it does things to my self-control when you loom over me.'

'Right, then, I'll sit.' She sat, gingerly, with a distance of three feet between them and that hectic colour still burning in her face.

'You might have to come close enough to see me.' He watched her do a reluctant bum-shuffle up the bed as though any sudden movement might launch her right into his arms.

'I'm moving closer.' She shuffled close enough that she could check his pupils, and that he could touch her if he moved his shoulder a little to the right.

People said the eyes were the windows of the soul. Luc wasn't sure he wanted Bella to take in that view in his just at this moment. Without thought, he lowered his eyelids, reached for her hand and clasped it instead.

If he saw it as a ploy to distract her, it worked. She gave a surprised gasp and dropped her gaze to those linked hands, but Luc hadn't planned it at all. Something inside had insisted he make the connection with her. That he have at least some small part of her in his possession. He suppressed a frustrated growl.

With her gaze lowered this way, Luc had a wonderful view of the planes of her cheeks, the long eyelashes that curled naturally beneath winged brows. And just enough of a hint of her mouth to make him…hungrier still.

Bella raised her gaze and looked right into his eyes. Searching for signs of any problems from the concussion? Yes, that would be part of it, but the vulnerability in her expression warned him it was a lot more than that.

'Do I have three pupils in each eye, or is everything normal?' His thumb stroked the back of her hand. He tried to inject playfulness into his tone of voice, and his expression.

'Nope. You only have one pupil per eye.' Her smile trembled. Soft lights danced in the depths of her eyes.

'I appreciate your willingness to stay tonight, to watch over Grace, and over me.' He drew a breath, drew in the scent of her and held it close. If he didn't let her go now, he might not want her to go at all. 'It's already heading for midnight. As you've seen for yourself, no harm has come to me. You could go home, Bella.'

It was the last thing he wanted.

Bella seemed to hesitate before she leaned towards him just the tiniest bit. 'I can't leave you, Luc, even if your "noggin" is in no apparent danger. I'd only stay awake all night and worry about you if I wasn't here.'

'Grace talked to you.' Naturally, his daughter talked with Bella. Luc had woken from a nap to hear the sound of their voices as Grace took her bath and got ready for bed. It had felt right then, to have Bella in his home doing those things with his daughter.

It still felt right and he wondered for the first time, could he and Bella have a chance together? If he made it clear he...liked her but would never be able to love her?

In the face of the more obvious problems, Luc had pushed aside the even deeper issues. But now some of those problems had resolved themselves. He knew the truth about Bella's last night in Milan. He suspected she had meant no harm in her arrangement with Maria although it had certainly been unfair to his aunt. Now Luc was forced to confront the things he had refused to think about.

Natalie and Dominic between them had ruined him for trusting in love again. Luc wished it were different, but it never would be. He simply had been hurt too much, and done too much damage himself as a result, to ever open himself to that sort of hurt again. He suppressed a humourless laugh. It seemed he and Bella were just like each other, in the end, very untrusting, for she certainly blamed him for his bad past behaviour!

Bella, unaware of his thoughts, spoke in a soft voice. 'I... enjoyed the evening routine with your daughter.'

Perhaps it was something in the way she looked, in her vulnerability as she sat next to him. Or perhaps he simply realised how much he wanted to keep her in his life.

But in that moment Luc realised he needed Bella on some level, and the only way to deal with that need was to tell her the truth—the whole truth—about his past so they could go forward from there.

He caught her gaze and held it. 'There's something I need to tell you.'

Luchino got up from the bed and pulled a bathrobe from behind the *en suite* door. After he shrugged into it and tied the belt, he returned to sit beside Bella.

Bella recognised the need for outer protective layers, employed it herself with the black catsuits she wore. They might fit like a second skin, but they also covered her from chin to ankle, and sometimes she had to have that. Not because of any physical restraint, but because of emotional ones.

Blood began to pump faster through her heart, her veins. What did Luc want to say to her? Was it something about them? If so, what, and how would she handle it, respond? She drew a deep breath. 'What is it?'

His mouth tightened into a harsh line that somehow revealed hurt, pain, regret and so much more right alongside his hunger for her. 'It's about Grace.'

Their hands were joined, and she didn't know when she had reached for him, or whether he had reached for her. When Luc stroked his thumb across the back of her hand she felt the churn of his emotion, and somehow that brought her own feelings closer to the surface, her own hurts and fears and the emotional uncertainty of recent months.

After one swift glance towards the opened bedroom door that led to the corridor and the bedrooms beyond, he released her hand, walked over and closed that same door. 'Grace isn't likely to wake, but if she does I don't want any chance that she might hear this. And I need to tell you, Bella. I want you…and I know we need to settle things between us.'

He paced the floor, and swung around to face her. 'That last night in Milan, after Natalie stormed up to our dining table and you learned she was my wife and you left us, she told me she agreed to terms of settlement so we could end the whole thing. She had a room booked in the motel and a lawyer waiting. We simply needed to sign.'

Bella tried not to reveal her surprise as Luc went on.

'Although a part of me wanted to go after you, try to explain, I couldn't do it straight away.' The frustration of those feelings seemed to swamp him, and her heart tripped in her chest.

Luc *had* cared that much, *had* wanted to set things right with her that night.

'I had to take Natalie's offer.' He bit the words out. 'I'd waited too long for it, and it meant securing Grace's future with me.'

'You wanted Grace with you even then?' Bella twisted her hands in her lap. 'But you left her.'

'Yes.' Just that one word held so much pain. 'There's no excuse for it, but I'll explain what happened. Natalie waited until the documents were signed and notarised by the lawyer, then she dismissed the guy, poured herself a drink from the room's mini-bar and toasted the biggest fool she had ever known.'

Luc's voice tightened with leashed emotion. The control he held over himself as he spoke made it clear how deep this had reached into his soul, his spirit.

'I—I don't understand.' Bella rose from her seated position on the bed, faced Luc, her hands clenched against the need to draw him to her, comfort him. Yet the instinct screamed inside her.

'I got married because, despite my precautions, Natalie was pregnant. I wanted to do the right thing by her and the baby. And then Grace arrived "prematurely".' He made quotation marks in the air with his fingers. 'Natalie made quite a song and dance of her fear for our child when she went into what she called early labour.'

If it hadn't really been an early labour…

Luc went on. He seemed determined to get it all out now that he had started.

'Big babies are common in my family, so Grace's average weight and size seemed about right, given she arrived what I believed was early.' Brackets appeared at the sides of Luc's mouth. 'In fact, she was born later than her real due date. She wasn't my child. Natalie was already pregnant with her when we met.'

'But why would she trick you, trap you into marriage when it wasn't your baby?' Bella saw it all in Luc's eyes. The horror of it, the hurt of it. She felt sick. That any woman could do such a thing to him seemed ludicrous to her. She couldn't fathom it, but Luc's wife had done exactly that.

'I don't know. To "keep it in the family", so to speak?' Luc gave a harsh laugh. 'Natalie gained great pleasure when she sent her lawyer off with the signed papers that yielded care of Grace to me, and then told me Grace was my brother Dominic's baby, not mine, that she was pregnant to Dom before our involvement began. I wasn't the richest, but Dom didn't come through as she expected. When she turned up pregnant from their affair, he refused to leave his wife and children and marry Natalie.'

'So she "settled" for you?' Outrage ate at Bella.

What must that have done to Luc's ability to trust anyone? A combination of rage on his behalf, empathy and shock made her tremble all over. 'Oh, Luc, I'm so sorry.'

A primal part of her wanted to find Luc's ex-wife and tell her just what she thought of her, possibly with physical, hair-pulling overtones. Bella was a long way from a *chai*-tea-induced calm right now! 'You must have been so upset that night.'

'I went after you to explain and ask you to stay, but I saw you coming out of the show manager's room.'

'And concluded I, too, had opted for whatever choice would work for me.' She wasn't angry any more over that. She was just…sad for him, for what he had gone through. 'It's all right, Luc. I understand how it must have looked to you.'

Luc nodded and swallowed.

And Bella tried to think through what Luc had told her. 'But the baby was Natalie's. Surely she wanted to keep her whether you were the father or not?'

'She got pregnant to trap Dominic into marrying her. The baby was only ever a ploy.' His mouth flattened. 'Natalie wouldn't even go near Grace after she was born. We fought about it until I realised I couldn't win. Then I fought to keep Grace with me because Natalie didn't want her or love her.

'I won that right.' He gave a harsh laugh. 'I got the baby. It's just that I also got the double betrayal of knowing Natalie only sought me out when Dominic refused to endanger his marriage by claiming the child as his own.

'And I confronted Dom about it later. He told me he couldn't help it if I was gullible enough to marry Natalie, and that it wasn't his problem if she got pregnant with his child during an affair that never had a chance of being more than that.'

Luc swung to face her, his face cast in shadow. 'I shouldn't have let it matter, but I allowed the betrayal of the wife I had tried to love, and the brother I had worshipped, to fill me with hurt, and I let that hurt drive me from Grace's side when she was innocent and helpless and needed me. After that night I lived in this kind of vacuum, driven forward only by my sense of betrayal and anger.'

'Oh, Luc.' Bella didn't know what to say to him, what to

feel. She wanted only to sympathise, but hearing him put this into words made Grace's abandonment all the more real.

'I got Grace a nanny, and walked away. I used the excuse of improving the family business all over Europe as my reason, but in my heart I knew the truth.' His eyes filled with pain. 'I checked on her once or twice a year, and every time I looked at her I saw *my* hurt, *my* pain and *my* needs. I convinced myself I didn't have *time* to see her more than that. I had work to do. Important work to help advance the popularity of exquisite jewellery around the world.' He spoke a low oath.

Bella trembled in reaction to his words. Her own hurt and pain flooded upward. She didn't want to blame Luc, could feel his heartache, but how could she accept this? 'Grace ran away.' It was the end of that part of the story, and maybe Bella just wanted to reach the end.

But Luc went on. 'Yes, I ignored the child I had claimed as my own. I made Grace so unhappy, so convinced her absence was the only thing that would please me, that she ran off.' His expression tightened even more as he seemed to revisit the starkness of that time. 'By pure happenstance I was in Italy when it happened. Even then, it took five hours from when I first learned of her disappearance to the moment I found her huddled in a shack on one of a number of small farms miles from where she started out.'

Bella didn't want to see his pain any more, didn't want the feelings rushing through her, the reminder of her parents' betrayal, her sisters' hurt. Her own.

But Luc swallowed and went on. 'She walked all the way, could have been snatched, run over, or could have starved to death hidden away before anyone found her. I betrayed my child, Arabella, just like your parents betrayed you.'

Luc flung the words out, harsh and low and filled with self-disgust. 'I decided to tell you this, hoping if you knew, we might be able to move past it and…have something together, but I was wrong, wasn't I? There's no getting past it. I don't know what I was thinking.'

Bella stared at Luc. She understood the grief behind his actions now, but it didn't blot out what had happened. 'I'm sorry, Luchino.' She backed to the door and moved through it. 'I'm sorry. Please understand I don't…I *understand,* but I can't separate myself from this.' What he needed was for her to say it didn't matter, but she couldn't do that.

Would he have made love to her if she had told him she didn't care about the past and agreed to that exploration? What was she giving up? But how could she *not* give this up, when each word he confessed deepened her hurt?

'I'll stay the night because Grace shouldn't be left without a second adult in case you get sick.' Bella could barely choke the words out through the lump in her throat. 'But in the morning, I'm leaving and…I want you to leave me to sell the rest of my gowns by myself. You know I won't stop until it's done, and it's best if…we don't see each other that way any more.'

'I guess I have my answer, then.' Jaw locked like granite, he turned away. 'As for the rest, I will still do what I believe is best for my aunt. If that means more functions to attend together, I'll expect you to comply.'

'Please reconsider.' She couldn't meet his gaze.

And Luc rubbed his head, sighed and looked away, too. 'I can't think about this any more right now. I'll let you know what I decide.'

CHAPTER ELEVEN

'I HAD CONSIDERED letting it all go, Arabella, but this invitation changes things in any case.' Luc dropped a thick vellum envelope into Bella's lap where she sat on the soft grass overlooking the Yarra River.

It was Monday lunch-time. They'd been apart less than two days and in that time Bella had agonised over him more than she had done six years ago. But no matter how she thought and struggled and stressed, no matter how she longed to wind back the clock and tell him yes, she wanted to be with him, that she could forget his past, Bella couldn't do that.

'You stayed away for two days, didn't call. I assumed you didn't want to work together on any more projects.' She climbed to her feet and faced him. When she looked into his grim face, her heart ached. Just the sight of him made her tremble, made her heart stutter and every emotion and feeling hidden deep inside flood to the surface.

Her fingers tightened on the envelope as she met guarded brown eyes in a face set in granite. 'How did you find me?'

'I stopped in at the store first. Hannah pointed me here.' He let his gaze rove to the skyscrapers beyond the river. 'Maria was busy with a customer.'

Bella preferred the sight of the water, the rolling green

of the lawns. Here in the sunshine with only a smattering of people around, it was as peaceful as anything could be since the night she walked out of Luc's bedroom, her emotions in turmoil.

Why did it feel wrong to have left him? She had nothing to offer him but a past riddled with the heartache of abandonment and she couldn't accept *his* abandonment of his daughter.

Even if Luc did care for Bella, they could never reconcile their differences. 'You shouldn't have come, Luc.'

'Do you think it was any easier to stay away?' He made a soft sound in the back of his throat. 'Can you possibly understand how my thoughts churn, how I ache inside when I think of you? Tell me you've thought of me, too.'

Day and night, constantly, until I think I will go mad.

'No. Please don't say…' She broke off.

Without looking at the envelope, she held it out to him. Drew a deep breath and tried to sound calm and professional. 'Thank you for bringing the invitation to me, but whatever it is, I don't want to participate.'

'We're invited to Milan, to the same fashion show that started it all six years ago.' He clasped the hand that held the invitation out towards him, pushed it inexorably back at her. 'Open it. Read it. Then tell me you can turn your back on such an opportunity for worldwide recognition for your gowns.'

'The same event?' How cruel could life be? Reluctantly, she lowered her gaze. The envelope had an airmail mark on it and no return address. When she opened the envelope and drew out the single sheet of paper, the sender's details leaped off the page. *Montichelli's.*

Not Luc's store, but the name of his family's jewellery business.

She had to read the words of the invitation twice before they made sense. Why would his family do this? Another thought occurred to her, and her gaze whipped to his face. 'Tell me you didn't ask for this.'

His harsh laugh mocked the possibility. 'The invitation came as a complete surprise to me.'

'Then why have they sent it?' They couldn't go. Why was she even asking? 'You cut yourself off from them. You're trying to start again, to be part of a family with Maria.'

He shrugged but his shoulders remained tight beneath the fitted black shirt. 'It's my goal to be strong competition to them in the market for exclusive handmade jewellery. Apparently they've had someone keep them informed of my progress here in Australia and now want to check my work more closely on their own territory.'

'Surely there's room for them *and* for you in the jewellery industry.' A hot rise of protective feeling crashed past her defences. 'They don't need to summon you back to Milan and inspect your wares.'

'They'll inspect your creations, too, and although their reasons may be less than altruistic towards me, it's to your credit that they want your gowns in the show. They only invite the best.' He pushed his hands into the pockets of his trousers.

Bella fought a surge of awareness, of hunger for him that hurt so much more now as she struggled to keep deep emotional feelings for him at bay. She lowered her gaze to the invitation again.

Luc's family had sent this invitation for all the wrong reasons. Why *should* he go back there when his brother had hurt him so much and his family had apparently let him leave Milan and not made any effort to help sort things out? 'Do your parents know about…Grace?'

'They wouldn't believe it if I told them.' His gaze drifted to the water. 'In their eyes, Dominic can do no wrong. It's always been that way.'

'Send a note to say we won't be there.' She didn't care less what the Montichelli family could do for her career. Luc was the only one she…cared about.

Which was another good reason to refuse the trip to Milan. That and the memories the trip would raise. Surely they would only wreak havoc on both of them. 'Or if you don't want to do that, I'll do it on behalf of both of us.'

'We're making the trip.' He said it with insistence in his eyes. 'You'll have your chance at world fame for your gowns.' A muscle twitched at the edge of his jaw and turbulence filled his expression.

'It would feel like you were selling out to them. I don't want to do that.' She didn't want to admit she cared, didn't want to be vulnerable, but she couldn't help it.

Luc gripped one of her hands in a firm clasp. 'I don't care about them. This is for you. I want you to take this chance.'

Oh, it hurt to touch him. Hurt and felt wonderful, all at once. She lifted a reluctant gaze and met the blaze of determination in his eyes, etched over his face. 'But—'

'No more arguments.' For a moment his tone softened and he looked right into her eyes. 'Please don't stop me from giving this to you. It's a chance of a lifetime. I want you to take it.'

Bella stared at him and fought the demand in his gaze, but in the end all she saw was the desire to do this for her.

'If it's what you want,' she whispered the words, capitulated with her heart without allowing her head a chance to think and decide against it, 'I'll go.'

This would be the final act, like the closing scene of a play. And maybe going back there *would* be the right way to end it. Maybe it would allow them both a closure they wouldn't be able to achieve here.

His sigh held relief as well as a release of tension. He gave a quick nod. 'This will be worthwhile for you, Bella. I know how things started out between us when I moved here, but believe it or not, your success is important to me now just because I want it for you.'

Because he cared for her?

She couldn't afford to think about that.

Before Bella could speak again, Luc turned to retrace his steps. 'I'll let Maria know what's happening so we can start preparations to attend. I'm sure she'll support the idea and allow you time to get everything ready.'

While Bella stared numbly, he started back across the wide green expanse of lawn.

You had no choice but to agree. First of all, he wouldn't have accepted no as an answer. And secondly, if he wants the chance to confront his family with his talent, you should support him in that. Do everything you can to help him *succeed.*

After a moment, Bella squared her shoulders and followed. She didn't care about herself. But for Luchino's sake, she would make the best job of this, ever. She would do him proud, spit in his family's collective eye—figuratively speaking—and then it would all be over between them.

She would have to leave her sisters again, but Bella realised for the first time ever she wasn't worried about it. Chrissy and Sophia could take care of each other if the need arose, and, with Nate watching so closely over Chrissy's health at the moment, her sister was in good hands anyway.

Right in the midst of the turmoil inside her, an odd feeling crept over Bella. She wasn't the only person who loved her sisters now. Nate loved all of them and would look after them as needed. That realisation felt quite strange.

'It's out of the question, this Milan trip.' Maria's voice rose and the words ran together as she continued. 'You mustn't go, Luchino. Bella, she mustn't go either. Nobody goes!' Rather than the tension of past weeks, Maria seemed to have progressed to full-blown panic.

Bella heard her boss's words and the distressed tone of them as she stepped over the threshold of the store and moved to stand at Luc's side. Fortunately there were no customers in the store right now, just the assistant, and Hannah had wisely made herself scarce among the racks of gowns at the back of the store.

'I take it Luc's let you know of our invitation to attend the Montichelli annual fashion show in Milan.' Even in the moments it took to retrace her steps to the store, the impact of the invitation began to sink in to Bella. They had only a few days to get ready if they wanted to make a good showing. Had Luc's family planned it that way deliberately, held the invitation back so he wouldn't have enough time to prepare properly?

'It's the chance of a lifetime for my gowns, Maria.' Bella moved to stand at Luc's side. Oh, it felt right to be there despite everything!

Luc cast a swift look towards her.

Bella returned his gaze without flinching. *I don't do things by half-measures, Luchino. If you want to go, we'll go, and I'll convince Maria that I'm dying to be there. Read the determination in my eyes!*

He gave one small dip of his head and a spark lit his eyes. It looked remarkably like admiration.

Maria turned flashing eyes on Bella. 'There's no need, and my Luc, he shouldn't have to show his jewellery to them. His talent is his own. He doesn't owe them anything!'

'Oh, Maria.' The older woman revealed so much of her affection for Luc in her protective words, and also a fear that related directly to her family. 'Luc and I have decided on this. I'm sure it will be OK.'

Bella let her gaze shift to encompass Luc, and climb until

she locked onto dark chocolate depths and held herself there. 'It's a great chance to get *Design by Bella* gowns into the international market. If Luc wants this, I'll do my best to be as successful at the show as I can be.'

And at the end of it, she would try to walk away with dignity. Somehow.

Luc's gaze softened. Tenderness crept into his expression, and Bella soaked it up. She couldn't stop herself.

'Luchino? You insist on doing this?' Maria's agitation showed in her quickened breathing, in the flush of her face and a tremble in the hands locked together in front of her. But she seemed to reach some sort of decision. 'I can't get you to change your mind?'

'I won't change my mind, but you don't need to worry about it.' He reached for Maria's clenched hands and held them in his. 'You'll stay here and take care of things while Bella and I make the trip. We'll be back before you know it. You won't have to…go near them.'

But Maria didn't relax and agree. Instead, she shook her head. 'If you insist on this, I'll go with you. They won't— If I'm right there— It's not me I'm worried about…' She dropped her gaze, withdrew her hands.

'Maybe if you told me what worries you?' Luc prompted his aunt, but Maria tightened her lips and shook her head and looked so torn that Bella's heart ached for the older woman.

Then, before Bella or Luc could speak again, Maria reached for the phone on the counter.

'We have a frantic few days ahead of us.' She seemed determined to throw herself into this, now the decision was made. 'Luc, go back to your store and choose the pieces you most want to display at the show. We'll do our best to combine them with appropriate gowns, but I'm sure you'll understand some compromise will be involved.'

Maria drew a breath before she turned to Bella. 'You, Arabella, go straight to the racks and mannequins and pull out everything you think you might want to use in the show. Any commissions you can finish between now and the trip will be modelled as well. I'll see what I can do to get someone to replace me in the store while we're both away so Hannah isn't left to cope alone.'

'OK, Maria.' Bella's concern for her boss began to fade as the reality of what lay ahead pressed in. 'I'll get straight to it.'

'Arabella, a moment of your time first, please.' Luc drew Bella away from Maria. His aunt's head was already busy with plans, even though she had opposed the idea of the trip at first.

Maria's concern and determination to attend seemed to contradict each other, but Luc wasn't entirely sure why. He would have to watch over her carefully during their time at the show. He didn't want anyone in the family upsetting her, although Luc wasn't sure what sort of reception he and his group would receive.

His brother would probably prefer to ignore him, might actually think Luc would give a damn if he did, and his parents? He hadn't heard from them since he moved to Australia. He turned his attention back to Bella. 'Can you get the same models we've already used? The ones who went with us to the Sydney fashion show?'

'I hope so. I'll contact them when you leave and I know if they possibly can, they'll say yes. It would be in their best interests to do the show, and I'm sure any agent would agree with that.' Bella drew a deep breath that didn't quite hide the well of excitement that made her eyes sparkle and a flush rise in her cheeks. 'It'll be a golden opportunity for them, as well.'

It pleased him to see her enthusiasm, because this was for her.

And for yourself, because you're not ready to let go of Bella yet and this is a way to keep her at your side longer.

That was true, even if he could see no way to maintain a relationship with her. Bella couldn't get past his treatment of his child.

If you could get beyond *that, would you now trust her enough to ask her into your life, into your...heart?*

To lay his heart completely open to someone else? Luc didn't know the answer.

'Your gowns will leave their mark on Milan.' *Feel excited about showing your creations, Arabella.* 'I want this for you, Bella. Everything else aside, I want you to have the pleasure of seeing your gowns modelled there. I want you to enjoy the appreciation and respect you get from the public and your peers.'

'It's different from being a model there, among so many others. This will matter a lot more, even if I try not to let it. I want to be a success for myself but also—for you.' She met his gaze and he saw her vulnerability, her care for him, and he wanted to pull her into his arms and *insist* they make a go of things.

But he didn't know if they could make it work, in fact, he felt certain they couldn't. Their pasts, separate and together, had robbed them of that chance. 'Grace and her nanny will come with us. I won't leave Grace behind while I go back to the country that held so much unhappiness for her. She might worry that I'd stay away from her again.'

'I admire the sentiment, but is it wise to take her among your family?' Bella lowered her voice, even though they were already speaking quietly. 'What if your brother sees her?'

'To return there then leave again with me—knowing she has me and nothing will change that—will be good for Grace.' Luc believed it, or he wouldn't take Grace back. 'Dominic won't try to even catch a glimpse of her. As far as he cares, I'm stuck with her and good riddance. So I'm not afraid for

Grace's emotional stability. I'll warn Heather to keep her away from the family, but there's really no reason any of their paths need to cross.'

'I guess they wouldn't recognise her, anyway. She'd just be a child with a nanny. Why would they even look at her?' Bella laid her hand on his arm. 'I see your point.'

He held her hand there and searched her face, her eyes. Had he slept at all since she left his room the night she came to watch over him? His body still longed for hers, and yes, his emotions reached out, too.

Bella's gaze flared in unexpected anger. 'I'd like to punch your brother in the kneecaps for his behaviour.'

She sounded as though she would do it, too. A smile crept up on Luc unawares, and spread across his face. Somehow, it brought healing to know she disliked Dominic, sight unseen.

'Get ready for the fashion show, Arabella.' He bent his head and pressed a swift kiss on her lips. He couldn't resist the temptation.

Heat spiralled through him as she clenched her hands and leaned into him. Maybe it was involuntary, but she did it, and Luc responded on a primal level.

His mouth had a will of its own. It gave itself utterly to the moment.

Don't wrap your arms around her. Don't beg her to stay safe in your embrace and try to keep her there forever.

'Prepare for the show.' He repeated the words, but this time they came in a gravelled undertone. 'Let me know if you need help with anything and I'll be there for you. I'll make it happen for you.'

And Bella warned him, 'This is the last event. When it's finished—' she stopped to draw a shaking breath '—*we're* finished.'

Luc refused to answer. He couldn't offer an assurance he wasn't sure he wanted to keep. If Bella showed any sign of softening, he might simply take whatever she was willing to give…

CHAPTER TWELVE

'WE DID it!' Lost in the moment, in the thrill of achievement, Bella allowed her excitement free rein. It seemed to reach all the way to the cathedral-style ceiling of the luxury hotel's lobby as she and Luc stepped through a velvet-draped arch and moved towards a small, secluded lounge area where they had arranged to meet Maria, Heather and Grace after the final presentation of Bella's gowns, and Luc's jewellery. 'Our designs were the most popular there.'

They'd been here for seven days of hard work, of appearance after appearance for the models. Tonight was the end, and Luc was glad. But Bella's happiness gave him a deep satisfaction and pleasure, and he wasn't ready to end his time with her.

She almost danced along at his side. Her hand gripped his arm and she leaned into him, caught up in the buzz of their success. The week had been fraught with worries, with concern about Maria's ever-growing unease, but also with the build-up of unspoken feelings between Luc and Bella.

He tucked her even closer to his side as the trio of Maria, Heather and Grace came into view.

A wave of longing washed over him. He wanted Arabella. He might not know how to keep her, might still not fully understand his feelings, but he knew enough to want her—

now—to want to be alone with her, to make love to her, to show her in a tangible way how much she meant to him.

'Once we've said goodnight to the others, we'll go out just the two of us, and show Milan how we can celebrate.' Luc wanted to show Bella more of this city than the snatches he had managed since they got here.

It all fascinated her. The historic buildings, the elaborate theatres and cathedrals, the ringing of the church bells.

After they celebrated in the arms of the city, he wanted Bella in *his* arms. 'Would you like to see something of the city at night with me? It's chilly, but we can help each other to keep warm and then later…' He hesitated, and then put it plainly. 'Later, I want to take you to my room and make love with you.'

She gasped. After a moment she drew a very slow, very deep breath. 'Yes. Yes.' Her face turned a rosier hue, and her voice dropped to a husky whisper, and Luc knew she understood all of his invitation, and wanted it, just as he did.

Awareness burned a trail over Luc's skin. He searched her gaze and found awareness, desire, confusion as well as excitement and…hope? Could he believe that was hope? Could he accept that hope?

Then Bella sobered to search his face. 'You haven't had another encounter with your brother? I lost track while I worked with the models behind the scenes tonight.'

'None since that first night when he admitted the invitation was his idea. With our parents away travelling, I doubt they even know I was invited.' Luc had sought Dominic out the first night to ask if he intended any trouble.

Dominic had been in the hotel bar and well on the way to drunk. His brother had refused to answer, but hadn't seemed to consider that Luc's designs might turn out to be better than the family designs on offer.

Luc couldn't help his pride at besting Dominic in this. 'I

caught a glimpse of him in the bar as we passed it just now. He seemed quite ensconced. If he invited me here simply to test the quality of my work, he's probably regretting it.'

'That's his problem.' Protective anger filled Bella's face. 'It serves him right that your jewellery received so much interest.'

When they drew level with the others, Maria couldn't seem to contain her smile. 'It went so well! Even from right at the back, I could see how well the gowns and jewellery were received.' Her smile faded a little as she searched Luc's face. 'You didn't meet me here as fast as I had expected. Nothing...unpleasant happened to detain you? I should have stayed, waited for you.'

'We wanted to congratulate the models and give them their bonus payments so they could enjoy a final night out.' Luc smiled as he held Bella against his side.

And I didn't want to risk having Dominic anywhere near you, Zia.

'Was it good, Papa? Do we go home tomorrow?' Grace's words held a hint of tiredness. It was past her bedtime, and Luc lifted her up with one arm around her and planted a kiss on her soft cheek.

His daughter wrapped her arms around his neck and squeezed, and he closed his eyes. His heart filled with gratitude for the bridges they had crossed in their relationship. 'It was good, and tomorrow we go home. If you get a good sleep tonight and eat a sensible breakfast, there'll be time for *gelato* before we leave for the airport.'

'Goody. I want *limone*.' Grace wriggled from his arms and grabbed Heather's hand. 'Let's go to bed. I'm very tired. I need a big sleep before morning.'

As Grace left the room with her nanny, Luc glanced at Bella and shared a smile. To his surprise, Bella wrapped her arms around him and hugged him hard.

'Your daughter becomes more confident and carefree every day.' Her mouth softened as she drew back. 'I don't think she has a doubt in her mind that her *papa* loves her.'

'Thank you for that.' Only Luc and Bella herself knew just how much her words meant. But was it enough for Bella to get past her own fears and memories?

'It's been a long evening and a long few days.' Maria seemed to tremble with pent-up feeling. 'I'm glad it's over. I've been so worried—'

'You have nothing to worry about.' Luc, too, had felt on edge, not entirely trusting Dominic's glib avoidance of his questions, and concerned that the return here would somehow harm Maria.

Now he stepped forward, took one of the shaking hands in his and wrapped his arm around his aunt's shoulders. 'You know you could tell me, Zia. About the past. I would do anything necessary to protect you from hurt or anxiety. *You're* my family, now, and I want you to trust me.'

Tears brimmed in Maria's eyes. She gripped his hand with clenched fingers. 'Luchino. I wanted to protect you, but I should have faced up to things, told you what I'd done when you first came to me in Melbourne. I was just so afraid you would be angry, reject me, and so I kept putting it off.'

Confusion and unease formed a leaden mass in Luc's gut. 'What do you mean, Zia?'

Maria's mouth trembled and she fought for words. 'I mean that I'm...that I'm your—'

'Well, well. What a cosy picture.' The words were slurred, angry, the voice instantly recognisable.

'Dominic.' Luc released Maria and stepped forward in an unconscious effort to shield his aunt and Bella from his brother's attention. When Dominic swayed on his feet, Luc's brows drew into a deeper frown. 'What do you want? You're drunk.'

Dominic took a step forward. His mouth twisted into a sneer. 'It was a fluke that your designs were the most popular at this show. You're still second best, and you always will be.'

'Second best to you, you mean.' Luc's hands clenched at his sides. Dominic seemed to want a fight. Luc didn't. 'Has it occurred to you that I don't care what you think, or what anyone else thinks? I'm past all that. I've moved on.'

'Don't you dare to call Luchino "second best" anyway. He's a better man than you will ever be.' Bella's low words sounded right beside Luc. Her hand gripped his arm hard enough to cut his circulation, and her statement warmed him even as Dom's fury seemed to rise.

'Leave Luchino alone.' Maria's words were half demand, half plea as she, too, chimed in to protect Luc, but he didn't need their protection. He simply wanted Dominic to leave before he upset either of them further.

'Better still.' Luc looked his brother over. Contempt and pity mingled. How could Dom have refused to claim Grace as his child? He had lost so much, and that loss was Luc's gain. He loved Grace with his whole life, all of his heart. 'Why don't you go home, brother?'

When Dom refused to budge, Luc turned to Maria and Bella. 'Go upstairs. I'll join you when I'm finished here.'

Bella's expression made it clear she didn't want to leave him, but she dipped her head and reached for Maria's arm. 'Let's go, Maria.'

'Good night, Zia. We can finish our talk tomorrow. Go straight to bed and don't worry.' Luc turned to Bella, the promise in his eyes for her alone. 'I'll see you soon.'

'She's not your aunt, Luchino.' Dominic's stark words filled the air, the vehemence of the announcement razor-sharp.

Bella hesitated, and then tried to encourage Maria away.

But Maria's face drained of all colour and she made a soft, panicked sound and couldn't seem to move at all.

Luc wanted to put his hands around his brother's throat and squeeze until the sneer fell away. Dominic had no right to hurt Maria, and he clearly had, even if Luc didn't understand Dominic's pronouncement.

What? Had the family formally divorced Maria years ago or something? Excommunicated her in legal terms? Luc's gaze went to his aunt, and again he felt that deep link to her. Whatever the truth, he wouldn't let Dominic hurt her.

'Leave, Dominic. Walk away right now and I may decide not to harm you.'

Bella tugged on Maria's arm. 'Come away, Maria. Let's go.'

Dominic simply stared at Luc. 'Poor, foolish Luchino. You never wake up, do you?' He glanced towards Maria before he turned back to Luc. 'You're the only one who doesn't know. Again. How does that feel?'

Luc stepped forward, reached for the lapels of Dominic's suit coat.

His brother stepped back out of reach, his laughter full of viciousness. Behind them Luc could hear Maria begin to sob as she begged Dominic in Italian to leave this, to let her be the one to tell Luc.

And Luc *did* feel like the fool, the only one who didn't know. Because Dominic had made this about Luc now, not only about Maria, and Luc didn't understand that. He snatched hold of Dominic's shirt front. This time his brother wasn't fast enough to move away. 'Tell me, then. Tell me this big secret that you think will cut me off at the knees.'

Dominic's bravado faltered in the face of Luc's anger. Then he lifted his hands and pried himself loose of Luc's hold. 'She's your mother, a whore no better than she should be. The family should have cast you both out. Instead our grandfather was weak. He kept you in the family because I was his only grandchild and he thought our parents should have two sons, just in case.'

The words scored through Luc's mind. At his side, Bella gasped. But even as he struggled to understand, Dominic went on.

His brother thumped his own chest with a fist. 'I was *enough!* But Grandfather insisted you be raised as my brother. You shouldn't have been there at all. Our parents always knew it. They resented you just for existing.'

One glance at Maria's face revealed all, and Luc felt as though a pit had opened up and swallowed him, burying him in darkness until he couldn't see, couldn't breathe. He was Maria's child. As he searched her face, he wanted his brother away from here, out of this.

'Leave, Dominic, right now.'

The other man started to laugh, until he looked into Luc's eyes. Then his laughter faded and fear flashed in his eyes before he tipped up his chin. 'The shoe is on the other foot, brother. I can hurt *you.* If this is not enough, I can take back the brat—'

'Luc!' Bella stepped in front of him, grasped the fist he had raised and closed her fingers over it. 'Can't you see he wants that? A nice public brawl to make you look bad. Don't give it to him.' Her gaze turned to Dominic, and as quickly dismissed him. 'He's just a sorry excuse for a man. You'd think he had enough on his conscience already.'

'I have nothing on my conscience at all.' Dominic lifted his head, glared without remorse but kept his distance from Luc. 'I'm a happily married man with three children growing up in my footsteps, and I can do what I want. You have no control over me, Luchino. I laugh that you would think you can command me—'

'Do you? Did you think I would leave things the way they

were and not take steps to protect *my daughter* and her interests, Dom?' Luc took a deep satisfaction from the unease that crossed his brother's face.

Bella was upset. Maria was crying, and Dominic had caused this. Now he would learn what Luc was capable of.

'Haven't you noticed the relentless buying of shares in your three key companies in the past five years? Each time you get in a financial hole, someone is there to buy a few more shares.'

Luc paused. 'Let's see. What were the most recent catalysts? Ah, yes. A hundred guests at a casino for a weekend with an open tab for all of them wasn't it? And before that, an exclusive world cruise for all your so-called friends?'

'How can you know this?' Dominic seemed to shrink in size in the face of Luc's revelations.

Bella stood silently at Luc's side, her hand still clasped over his. She held Maria's hand, too, and the older woman had stifled her tears and now glared at Dominic with cold fury.

Luc took his time before he answered Dominic. Instead, he took his fill of Bella's loveliness, her stalwart support, before he turned to his brother and said, finally, 'Through financial management I've bought enough shares in your businesses to make life very unpleasant for you should you ever think of trying to hurt me, Maria, *or any other member of my family* again. Do you understand me, Dominic? Try anything to hurt those I love, and *I will hurt* you.'

Dominic tossed off a stream of furious words, turned and stumbled away. But he understood. With his shoulders slumped, and his head bowed, he looked a very different man from the one who had dropped Maria's secret at Luc's feet and waited for Luc to fall apart at the news.

Luc turned back to Maria's tearful face, and Bella's anxious one. Now that Dominic was gone, Arabella's face also revealed her shock and confusion.

'Let's get Zi—*Maria* to her room.' His primary thought was to get Maria away from possible prying eyes. 'This isn't the place…'

'I agree, and Maria must give you an explanation.' Bella kept her tone soft, but Luc could sense the boil of emotions beneath the surface. Did Bella blame Maria for leaving him? Would it seem just one more insurmountable fact to Bella, something else to stand between them?

And did *Luc* blame his…mother? Even if he knew everything and wanted to blame her, he was the last person to have that right. 'Let's give Maria a chance to compose herself and give that explanation.'

'I will. I promise you, Luchino.' Maria tried to say more, but again emotion choked her words.

After that they made their way to Maria's room in a silence loaded with feeling, but no words were spoken. Luc didn't know what to say, what to think or hope for or try to prepare for.

When they arrived outside her room, Maria opened the door and gestured them both inside. Her hands shook, she remained pale, but she seemed determined to finally speak out.

Bella shook her head. 'I don't want to intrude, and I'm not sure I want to hear anything more. My sisters and I…' She stopped. 'You and Luc should settle this between yourselves.'

'But Luchino needs you at his side.' Maria's head lifted and pride and humility warred on her face. 'Whatever you think of me, Arabella, whether you condemn me or not, I want you to be here for…my son.'

Luc frowned at Maria's words, was about to speak, when Bella replied.

'Please forgive me, Maria. This is a struggle for me because it reminds me of my own past and I feel…protective of Luc, but I want to have an open mind towards you.'

Luc realised then that they had a lot to sort out. He and

Maria, he and Bella. He turned to the woman who now meant so much to him. 'Please stay.'

Bella finally nodded and they all moved inside. There were three chairs and a small table. They sat, and he leaned forward to try to put Maria at her ease. Bella sat to his right, her hands locked in front of her.

After a second, she moved her chair closer to his and reached for his hand. He took it, squeezed, and gave Maria the most encouraging glance he could manage. 'What happened, Maria? How did you end up in Australia, and I end up in Dominic's family when I wasn't his brother?'

'It was as Dominic said.' Maria clasped her hands tightly together and her gaze moved between him and Bella.

The tortured expression Maria carried revealed all the strain of the past weeks since he had pushed his way into her life and Luc was suddenly afraid she wished he hadn't. 'You became pregnant…out of wedlock?' Back then, it would have been a big deal, he knew.

'Yes.' Maria's lips trembled but she fought back tears. She seemed determined to tell it all without breaking down.

Luc's heart began to pound as he tried to accept she was his mother, and had carried that secret, would possibly have carried it to the grave if he hadn't sought her out. 'Why? Why did you let me go and never try to know me? At least later you could have—'

'Give her a chance to explain.' Bella's soft admonition stopped his words, and he saw the caution and shared pain in her eyes as they sought his. This wasn't easy for her, yet she wanted Maria to have a chance to express her reasoning.

Bella had grown, had changed over the past weeks whether she realised it or not. Had she changed enough to accept him, his history and all, and love him despite it? Luc's heart thudded as he realised he wanted Bella to do so.

'You were conceived when I was sixteen, Luchino.' Maria whispered the words with her gaze downcast, but then she lifted her head and looked at him very directly and let him see the years of bottled grief and pain. 'I thought I was in love, but the family bought your father off, he left the country and left me alone. They gave me a choice.

'Hand you to Dominic's parents when you were born, move away, and never see you again, or they would make it impossible for me to get work or help anywhere in Italy if I tried to keep you. I had no money, no hope…'

No hope but to let him go. It was still unpalatable, but Luc realised his grandparents were at fault, not Maria.

'They were monsters to do that to you, Maria. That must have been so hard for you.' Bella's soft words filled the silence. Not a complete acceptance, perhaps, but the beginnings of one as she realised *Maria* had been hurt—been made a victim.

'They bought me a ticket to Australia.' Maria sent Luc another regretful look. 'Over the years I worked hard and finally built up a business of my own, but I also spent money to console myself in the dark hours, and across those years that habit proved very hard to break.'

'Then I showed up in the world you'd rebuilt, and caused you even more distress.' Yet he couldn't be sorry.

Maria leaned forward to grip his free hand. 'Only because I didn't know how to tell you the truth and I so wanted to reveal it and beg to be allowed to be your mother again!'

Bella pushed her fist to her mouth, and somehow they were all on their feet and Luc had Maria's hand in his as Bella pressed her shoulder against him in the way he had seen her touch her sisters, a show of solidarity that wrapped around his heart and squeezed even as that lonely place inside him that had ached for family, to feel as though he belonged, trembled.

'You went to Australia and made a success of your life.'

He hesitated and cleared his throat against a sudden tightening. 'But you never tried to contact me.'

That hurt, he acknowledged, and pressed his shoulder back to Bella's because she had hurt that way when her parents walked away, had felt that same pain and so much else besides.

'I wrote to Dominic's parents. They told me you were happy, a joy to them, loved and content and secure.' Maria's eyes begged him to forgive her. 'I didn't want to threaten your happiness. Then later, when you were a man, I felt...I had no right to try to make my way back into your life.'

She gave a small, sad smile that tugged at his remaining defences. 'When I heard your message on my phone machine, I could barely comprehend it, but I was afraid to meet you, afraid you already knew what I'd done and hated me and only wanted to tell me so. But you weren't happy with them, were you? I'm so sorry.'

Tears fell on her lined cheeks, and Luc couldn't bear it any longer. He pulled his aunt, his *mother,* into his arms and only as he did, realised Bella too had reached out and they both had Maria tucked safely in their hold.

This could be right, couldn't it? A new start? They could go ahead, him and Maria, and it would be a good thing? 'Don't cry, Zia, *Mamma.* I'm not angry.' He swallowed hard and tightened his hold on her. 'I'm not angry. I understand. I've...done things, too. I'll explain about them, one day.'

But not now, because it was clear that Maria had taken all she could cope with.

Bella must have realised it, too, because she stroked a hand over Maria's arm and said quietly, 'You're grey with tension and exhaustion. I think it would be a good idea if you rested now.'

Luc agreed, and he wanted Bella's arms around him in private. Wanted to wrap her close and breathe her scent and release the tumultuous feelings that still held him hard in their

grip. He had a mother. It was wonderful and odd and unbeliev-
able, but it was great. He would make sure it worked for them.

He released his hold on Maria, but kept her hands in his.
'I can still be your son for a very long time, if you wish that
new relationship.'

'Yes. Yes.' Maria burst into tears again, and he held her and
rocked her in his arms for a long time, swallowing hard before
he finally let go. 'Go to bed. Promise you'll rest and not worry
about anything. What happened tonight is good. The future
will be good, too. We'll make it so.'

Maria's mouth trembled but she sniffed and wiped the
tears from beneath her eyes. The tension seemed to drain
from her at last. 'I will like that very much.' She hesitated, and
a tremulous smile formed. '*My son.*'

'Good—goodnight.' Luc was afraid he would unman
himself and break down utterly. Somehow he made it to the
door and, as Bella hugged Maria and said her goodbyes, he
drew deep breaths and pulled himself together.

To a degree!

When Bella joined him and they stepped into the corridor,
he reached for her hand and a sigh of relief escaped him as she
clasped it. 'I don't want to go out. I want—I need to hold you.'

'It's what I need, too.' Bella made the admission, and knew
it came from the depths of her heart.

In Maria's room, as Luc struggled through Maria's revelation, Bella had a realisation, too. She loved him. She had
loved him for six years and that love that had begun then was
now so strong, so full and complete, it possessed all of her.
Heart, mind, spirit, body. All wanted Luchino, needed him,
needed to show him those feelings, to give them freely.

'I have to tell Grace the truth.' Luc burst out with the words
as they turned into the corridor that led to their rooms. His
came first, and he stopped outside the door, his hands

clenched. 'Others know and I can never fully protect her from the chance of someone telling her. She has to hear it from me.'

Bella stopped, too, and a flood of memories of another time in this hotel crept up on her.

But she pushed them aside because they were only memories. Yes, they built a foundation of feeling in her for Luc, but this was now, this was real. And Luc was suffering for his daughter, fearing for her. 'Grace is still young, and she's been afraid. I don't know if she's ready…'

'No. Not yet.' He seemed to realise it, too, but his determination remained firm. 'But when she is ready, when she feels secure, I will tell her and explain it so she knows and can't be hurt by it.'

'Yes.' A deep hunger for Luc welled inside Bella and threatened to flood everything else away. She wanted to comfort him, to take him to her heart.

He lifted a hand to trace the curve of her cheek.

Bella pressed her face into his palm, seeking more of him. When she looked into his eyes, awareness and hunger beckoned, but also something different, much deeper, and filled with the same vulnerability and hope she felt? It seemed so, and her heart raced even as she warned herself this was *not* all resolved.

Unlike Luc and Maria, *Bella and Luc* had not fixed all their issues. But Luc must trust her now, mustn't he? And she accepted that he hadn't set out to hurt his child, that pain had fuelled his actions and he later came to regret them. That was all they needed, wasn't it?

Bella didn't want to *discuss*. She wanted to *show* Luc, in his arms, all that she felt for him. If her heart warned there was more that she was ignoring, she refused to heed it. 'Take me inside, Luchino. You said you needed to hold me. I want you to do that.'

Her hand rose to his chest, above his heart, and rested there. Beneath her fingertips, his heart raced.

'*Dio,* Arabella, my beautiful one.' He trembled as his hand rose to touch her face, to trace her lips. 'Do you know what you're accepting?' His arms banded around her. Long fingers stroked the bare skin of her back, revealed by the cut of her gown.

For tonight she wore a shimmering russet gown with finest spaghetti straps, a fitted bodice that moulded perfectly to her breasts, and left half her back bare. The feel of Luc's hands there incited a deep well of hunger inside her, a determined hunger deaf and blind to all warnings even if she had wanted to listen to them. She pressed her lips against his ear. 'Nothing will happen between us tonight that we don't both want.' She couldn't even remember his question, or maybe she didn't want to think of it.

With a low growl, Luc drew his room key from his pocket, unlocked the door and shoved it open, then ushered her inside.

A lamp burned on the telephone table. The curtains were open beside a bank of windows. Outside, old buildings met with new to fill the skyline with the grandeur of the city. Bella could only see Luc. Only wanted Luc.

He took one step in her direction, just one, and stopped with his hands clenched. 'I want to make love to you, to be heart-to-heart with you and never let go. Do you understand, Bella?'

Again that push for acknowledgement, and again uncertainty tried to raise its head, but Bella could see nothing, hear nothing but the man before her and the drumbeat inside her that insisted she be with him now. 'I don't blame you for what happened with…with Grace. And…I want you so much. I need your arms around me, to hear your heart beat with mine.'

'Bella, *mia cara.* How I've longed for you.' He caught her in his arms, pressed her against him from cheek to thigh, inhaled against her neck.

She felt the movement of his lashes at her temple as he let his eyes drift shut, but more than that she felt the tremble in his arms, the thunder of his heartbeat against hers as they pressed together.

If something inside whispered that she didn't entirely trust him, it must be wrong, mustn't it? Bella pushed all thoughts away. 'Please, Luchino. Make love to me.'

CHAPTER THIRTEEN

'I WILL make love to you with all I have in my heart to give, Bella *mia*.' Luc whispered the promise into Bella's golden hair. So much had happened, he still felt on edge, his emotions raw while hope rose in his heart for a future with his mother.

Was it greedy to want Arabella, too? Because desire for her brought hunger and tumult, longing, need. And love was above it all. He gazed into her face and allowed the knowledge to finally rise inside him.

Yes. He loved her.

God knew, he probably had loved her from the first night he saw her, right here in this hotel six years ago. An ill-fated love then, but could he take a chance on it now and hope that Bella had grown enough and could trust enough to open her heart to him? She *seemed* to be ready, seemed to…care.

'I have a need that nothing but making love with you will satisfy, Arabella. I admit it.' Truth rang in each word. His hands shaped her back, pressed into the dip at the base of her spine. Her body arched into his, touched his at heart, hip, thigh.

'Let me show you…' And maybe as he held her, she would also understand the feelings he wasn't sure he could express in words. The part of him that only made sense when he was with her, the deep need for her that even now terrified him because it ripped up his control and left him defenceless in her hold.

But he couldn't walk away. He had to have this, have her, and he bent his head and gave to her in feeling and sensation what he couldn't yet say.

'Luc. I…need you.' The words struggled up from a deep place in Bella's heart. She burned for him with a physical hunger, but that was only the start. Her heart cried out for him and, even as that terrified her, Bella had to reach for him.

'Then touch me. Feel the way I burn for you.' Luc lifted her hand, pressed it to his chest. His gaze burned into hers, too, and Bella felt…

Hot skin. A strong heartbeat, one beat after the other just as Melbourne's Yarra River flowed, its current constant, true. In the same way Milan stood strong and proud, a mixture of heritage, history and life.

Luchino was strong, and sometimes that strength made him ruthless, but he had a core of goodness that he had shown tonight. That he had already shown to Bella in other ways, too. She had asked him to leave her. To walk out of her life and stay out.

At that knowledge, she gasped aloud because how could she ever be without him? In this instant, it seemed impossible. Her body pressed closer to his heat and his hunger. Her heart reached for him, too. 'I want to touch you, Luc.' *I need to and if I can't, I think I'll die.* 'I don't want to have to stop.'

He gave a rough half-laugh that sent a shiver down her spine. 'I burn for you. Inside and out until I can't think about anything but you.'

Clothing fell away—his jacket and shirt, her dress. Beneath the dress she wore only panties and stockings held up by sheer black garters. He cupped her breasts, lowered his head and kissed her there. She closed her eyes and let sensations wash over her. Each touch worshipped her body. Each murmured word praised, let her know how much he wanted and needed her.

Luc led her into the bedroom, paused to stroke shaking fingers down her cheek and kiss her with exquisite tenderness. He removed the last of their clothing and wrapped her close in his arms. As he lowered her to the bed he looked into her eyes, and for a moment, such light reflected in the depths of his eyes...

'Luc?' Her hands trembled, so she locked them around his neck. Her mouth trembled, so she pressed it to his cheek.

'Hush. Just let me love you.' Dark eyes locked with hers and a current of deep hunger passed between them, a hunger for more than physical joining, and *that* was what frightened her. Did he know it?

Bella wondered at that connection, too, and then she couldn't think any more as he wrapped her in an embrace that seemed to encompass all her hopes and dreams and fears and needs. 'I've never...'

He seemed to know. His eyes widened and a fierce look of possession and determination filled his face.

'Bella. *Dio.*' He braced above her. His arms trembled as he searched her face. 'You are so beautiful. I want to worship your body until you cry out for me...'

He proceeded to do just that, brought her to the brink of passion's end, until she thought she could feel no more, and then he brought them together utterly and those feelings built and built again before finally they splintered all around her. Her heart, her emotions, her thoughts, all shattered as Luc's broken cry filled the air and he, too, fell.

When it ended, he held her in his arms and she knew nothing in her life before had prepared her for this, and nothing that came after would ever be anything like it.

He stroked her back, his long fingers gentle and possessive

against her skin. As their bodies cooled, he drew the quilt up. It settled over them with a whisper, cocooned them in warmth.

Bella curled against his side and fought a sudden rush of panic as she faced all this had meant to her, and realised that loving him stripped her of all control, left her utterly defenceless to him.

'What is it?' He wrapped his arm around her and hugged her tight, and Bella couldn't tell him of those fathomless fears.

Not now when she couldn't face them or think of them, herself. 'It's nothing. I'm fine.'

He drew her body back into the shelter of his arms, cocooned her in his strength and tenderness until tears welled up and she had to force them back so he wouldn't know. Lethargy came and they fell asleep, spooned together with Luc's body wrapped behind hers, his mouth pressed to her hair as he held her, and she...wanted to be held by him.

In the morning while the shadows still held the night and before dawn touched the city, they showered together. With his gaze locked on hers, Luc washed her body. She couldn't look away from the intensity in his eyes, from the promises and determination she saw there.

Her heart lifted, oh, it lifted so dangerously, so temptingly. At the same time, the fears that sought for voice last night rose, and would not be denied. To love Luc, to accept her feelings for him, would mean such vulnerability. She would give her heart to him and what if he hurt it?

And could she embrace his child and love Grace as she ought? Or would she again be overwhelmed by feelings of inadequacy, by an inability to give any more?

That kind of commitment was unrelenting, consuming. It left no room for fear or fallibility, and Bella *had* stretched her reserves as she guided her sisters through the aftermath of the desertion of their parents.

Luc seemed troubled this morning, too. They dressed and ate the early breakfast he ordered, while light forced its way through the gap between window and curtain, and the world started up for the new day.

Luc set aside the cup that held the remains of his coffee, and turned on the sofa to face her. His expression held a raw kind of determination that...scared her.

Bella got to her feet, wrapped the hotel bathrobe more firmly around her. 'I should go. We leave today—'

Luc got to his feet, too, and said calmly, almost without expression yet with *so much expression:* 'I'm in love with you, Arabella. I have been for a long time. Last night I accepted it, and I don't believe making love was only a physical expression for you, either. I believe you have feelings for me, deep feelings. I want those feelings, whatever it costs.'

Could he really mean what he said? Oh, she wanted to believe it but her past held so much loss, her heart had suffered, and now when she wanted to trust in him and trust in her ability to return his love, to be strong enough to let him have her emotions, the care of her feelings, she realised she couldn't.

All those odd, lost, uncertain feelings of panic and emptiness and unease welled up and she knew they had all led to this, to a challenge to yield all, to love utterly and be vulnerable wholly.

Bella felt ill inside because she truly believed she couldn't do it.

'Please. This is too much. I can't—' She broke off. And even in her panic, she asked, *did he really love her?* Bella wanted to hug the hope close, wrap herself in it, but she couldn't.

'Last night was wonderful.' She whispered the words and tried not to think of the loss of his touch, the empty nights ahead. It was better to stop this now, before she really learned to believe in him and before her deficiencies were exposed to him. 'I didn't know it would lead to this. You made it clear you would never commit to a woman again.'

'I think you knew I'd changed.' He watched her face. Did he see her love?

Fear rose in a strangling tide. 'I—I can't... We have to go back to Australia, to real life.' And Bella wanted to leave right now and not stop until she got to her room in the flat and locked the world out and just stayed there and stayed there. 'This was just...'

'It wasn't *just*.' Anger burned in his eyes, but hurt burned more and she couldn't look at him.

Couldn't. His love! It was all her heart had longed for six years ago. In this very hotel she had built dreams, piled them up to the clouds. She wanted his love even more now than she had then, but... 'I can't change who I am or how I feel. I can't give you the love you want, Luc.'

Unconditional, unlimited love. That was what Luc wanted and she wanted him to have it, but it wouldn't come from her. She couldn't give that because she was broken inside.

Too many thoughts! She forced them all away and went to the door, shoulders curved, arms longing to wrap protectively around her middle.

'What happens now, Arabella?' He faced her with his hands clenched at his sides. His body radiated tension and his eyes bored into hers, demanded answers she couldn't give.

Pain lodged in her chest, a hard, heavy weight because she didn't want to lose him, and she knew she would. 'We end it. I know you'll be part of Maria's life and I respect and support that. I'll speak to Maria about doing more of my work from home. I'm sure we can work things out so I go to the store less often. Our paths shouldn't have to cross too much.'

Luc glared. 'You're determined to throw this away, despite everything that's happened.' His mouth tightened. 'You're not a teenager or young adult trying to cope with abandonment any more. You're a living, caring, *loving* young woman, capable of commitment if you choose it.'

He strode to the door, opened it and stood back. 'All I can believe is that you don't choose it.' He didn't try to keep her there, to touch her, hold her, and oh, Bella wanted and needed his touch, his arms around her.

Get used to it. This is your future, every day for ever.

'I won't regret last night.' It was her turn to tilt her chin, to stare into his eyes and defy him to contradict her. 'It was the most beautiful experience of my life and I'll never forget it.'

'But you don't love me enough to stay.'

She couldn't respond. Her heart breaking, Bella moved through the opened door, and walked away.

For three days and nights Bella barely ate, didn't sleep and couldn't talk to her sisters. She never knew she could hurt so much. Each day at *Maria's* was a strain as she wondered if Luc would enter the store, braced to see him, to cope with her longing and accept her decision.

Maybe one day he would find someone who could love him as he deserved.

Her heart ached afresh at the thought, and the sandwich she had brought to eat beside the quietly flowing river was returned uneaten to its wrapper.

When Bella saw a little girl run towards a small bridge that spanned a still eddy of backwater from the river, she watched for a moment before she realised it was Grace, and gasped aloud.

It was Saturday afternoon, the store closed for the day, and Bella had come here to think, to try to find some peace before she went back to the flat, to Sophia's concern and her own growing unhappiness.

Bella turned her head, and gasped again as Luc's long strides came to a stop right beside the park bench.

'Hello, Arabella.' Without waiting for a reply, he sat on the bench beside her. 'I hoped I might find you here.' He sounded calm, but a muscle flexed in his jaw and his hands were clenched where they rested on his thighs.

'I've come here a lot lately. I can't seem to exercise, or drink tea, and sewing is my work now...' She couldn't seem to do any of her usual things to try to get rid of the great ball of tension and unhappiness lodged deep inside. Even when her parents had left, Bella couldn't remember feeling this low. 'Why did you come here, Luc? Wouldn't it be better to just stay away?'

'I've made mistakes in life, Arabella. I've survived the betrayal of a wife and brother only to hurt my daughter, the one I most needed to protect.' His hands clenched even tighter. 'I don't want this, *us,* to be a mistake, too. We're made to be together, you and me. If you could just trust me—'

'I want to.' All her love for him welled up and she gave a broken laugh. 'I want to be with you.' In a recess of her mind she noticed Grace moving off the bridge and back onto the grassy knoll, but Bella's thoughts were fixed on this. For the first time, she admitted *the rest* of her fears.

'I have nothing to give to...a family. For months I've struggled to get control over my feelings, have felt drained and unhappy and disconnected in some way.

'I...I love you, Luc, *so much* that sometimes it hurts to just breathe and know you aren't there. And I care about Grace and I *want* to be in both your lives, but memories of my past struggles, or what it was like to try to give so much, love so much, scare me. What if I committed to you, and couldn't be a good mother to your daughter?'

She faced him, her heart fully open to him in this moment.

'What if I wasn't enough for you? If I let you down somehow? If you didn't want to be with me any more? What if I gave and gave, and then there was nothing left to give?'

'I will always want you and love you, Arabella.' His words held the same ring of truth they had when he spoke similar ones to his daughter. 'And while you're giving, I'll be giving, too. We'll fill each other if you'll let me give that support to you.'

'I don't understand.' But suddenly memories rose in Bella's mind. Of Chrissy, angry and determined the first time she had brought home a pay cheque.

Let me give all of it into the family coffers, Bella. I know what I'm doing. It's my decision.

And Soph, still in school, lost, scared, but determined to carry her share of the emotional load.

Tell me how you felt when our parents left, Bella. You never talk about it. I could give you a hug.

Only in the last few months had Bella allowed the cracks in her composure to show—even a little—to her sisters. She had carried them and loved them, but placed limits on what she let them do in return!

'I've locked everyone out.' The realisation washed over her. 'I've been so busy trying to keep myself safe that even when I tried to keep my sisters safe, I still didn't entirely let them in.'

But Bella could open up and let others in. She was strong. She could do it. She *could*. It wasn't a case of inability, of a limited amount of love. It was fear, pure and simple, and she had to be stronger than that, had to let the fear go.

Hope rose in her. Had Grace's young heart lifted with hope, too, as Bella's did right now?

'Take a chance on us, Bella.' Luc's words implored and commanded her. 'Caring for your sisters was hard on you, a huge responsibility. I know it took from you, but you love them. You're already learning to receive their love back to let *them* fill *you*. There's a deep bond between the three of you that will never be broken. Have you thought about that? You and I could build that bond together, too.'

The expression in his eyes insisted she consider his words, and believe him. 'Accept my past as a part of me, but let *me* pay for it myself. Don't punish me when it's up to me to face it and answer for it.'

And Luc *had* answered for it, and paid for it, every day, day after day. Those lost years were a blot on his soul that might never really heal, and all Bella had done was heap condemnation on top of it all. As if she had the right!

'Oh, Luc. Forgive me.' She whispered the words. 'I—I know you'll never let Grace down again. I want you to forgive yourself for that, and please, I want to say yes to you.'

Yes to Luc, yes to Grace, yes to everything. If it was difficult, so be it. If she hurt and ached when things were troubled, if she wondered how they would go forward and if they would survive, Luc was right. They would be there together. They would face it all together.

'A mother to Grace.' She murmured the words, embraced the concept for the first time. Her heart had longed to love the little girl. She turned to Luc, to tell him she would be the best mother she could possibly be, that she already loved Grace, if he could just forgive *her!*

'I can live with a nanny again.'

The words, spoken in Grace's young voice, brought Bella's head up.

Luc's daughter stood not far from them, a solemn expression in her eyes. 'I want you and Papa to be happy. I'll go away with Nanny Heather if that's what you want.'

'It's not what I want! It's not what your father wants, either.' The last of Bella's concerns gave way to a welling of love for the little girl. She got to her feet, reached for Grace, and when Grace allowed it lifted her into her arms.

Soft arms wrapped around her neck, and Bella gave a gentle squeeze as she buried her face in the child's dark, glossy hair. 'I want to be part of your family, Grace, to love you and your *papa*. I want us all to be together forever. I was just scared I wouldn't be able to make you and your dad happy.'

Grace drew back in Bella's hold, looked into her face and seemed to read truth there. 'I won't go away, then. I'm not sure my *papa* would have let me, anyway.' A tentative grin broke through. ''Cause he told me he wants me forever and ever.'

Bella swallowed and eased the little girl to her feet. 'Your *papa* doesn't want to ever let you go, and that's exactly as it should be.'

Grace turned to her father. 'I get to have a new *mamma* after all, then, don't I? I get to have Bella as my *mamma*.'

'Yes. Yes, you get to have a new *mamma*.' Luc's words were hoarse with emotion. He, too, hugged his daughter, and seemed almost at a loss as to what to do next.

Grace took the responsibility from him with a long-suffering huff. 'I'm going back to *the bridge*. I'll stay there and look for ducks for *a long time*.' She leaned forward, tugged his arm until he bent his head so she could whisper loudly into it. 'I think you should kiss her, Papa. It worked when the frog wanted the princess.'

'Thank you, Grace. I'll keep that in mind.' Luc's expression remained composed as he watched his daughter skip away to the small bridge again.

When he turned back to Bella, she couldn't help it. A grin spread across her face. 'There are worse fates than being compared to a frog, you know.'

'I know.' He reached for her. 'Come here. Maybe you can turn me into a handsome prince.'

Bella received his kiss, and opened all of her heart to him as she returned it. After long, drugging, emotional moments, Luc lifted his mouth from hers, and she smiled into his eyes, her mouth trembling a little despite herself.

'Whatever is in front of us, we'll face it together.' Luc made the pledge to her.

In the deepest part of her heart, Bella acknowledged the truth of it. 'I'm sorry I let my fears stand between us. I can't bear the thought of not being with you, Luc. You're deep in my heart and soul. You always have been. It's simply taken me this long to accept and admit it.'

'Bella, my love.' Luc glanced beyond them.

Bella followed his gaze. His daughter stood on the small bridge, her back turned, but she sneaked covert glances over her shoulder that she probably thought they couldn't see. Bella smiled. 'She's safe. I don't think she'll move from there until we go get her.'

Luc paused, reached into the pocket of his trousers and withdrew a small velvet pouch. 'It's not a conventional ring, but it holds my dreams for the future with you.'

Luc drew the ring from the pouch and held it between thumb and forefinger, his gaze fixed on her face. 'Say you'll marry me, Bella. I've waited so long.'

Her vision blurred, emotion clogged her throat, but she blinked the tears back and let her gaze shift to the ring he held between them. It was a shimmering *cloisonné* enamelwork set in a framework of delicate knotted gold.

Each strand of gold wrapped around the other, twined together and rose to clasp the gorgeous design. 'It's beautiful. With each shift of the light, I see more depths, more colours.'

'Our lives will be the same. Richer for the time we spend

together, stronger for our joining.' He slipped the ring onto her finger, cupped her chin and lifted her face to his. 'You haven't said it.'

'I'll marry you.' Her hand lifted to rest above his heart. Her spirits lifted to embrace all the hope their future together could hold. 'Oh, yes, I'll marry you!'

He swept her into his arms, kissed her until her senses swam and she longed for him in every part of her.

When he drew back, he looked into her eyes and his narrowed a little. 'I'm accustomed to having my way, to taking charge. Sometimes I'll fight you for control.'

'I like control, too, but I'm learning sometimes it has to be shared, or even yielded for a time to someone else. There's trust involved in that, and I do trust you, Luc.' Her fingers moved against his chest, and she raised her brows in question. 'You used to carry something here, against your heart.'

'My photo of Grace.' His mouth softened as he turned to look towards his daughter again. 'After she ran away, I never wanted to forget her, even for a minute. I keep the photo in my wallet now. As you saw the night we took our models out for a meal. And I've realised she's in my heart for all time whether I have any reminders close by or not.'

'You're in my heart the same way.' She realised it was true. Luchino was her one and only. He always had been, and always would be. On her finger, the ring sparkled in the sunlight. Bella knew this work, the rare designs, only a handful of which were available in the world. 'How did you know?'

'The hand-sewn gown. Maria showed me, told me how much you liked the *cloisonné* work.'

Luc had taken the work of a master craftsman and made it into something even more unique and special for her. Bella glanced across to the bridge and discovered Grace had given up all pretence of ignoring them. The little girl danced up and down on the spot, all but bursting with hope and excitement.

'I want more just like her.' The words burst from her and she realised she could have Luc's child, maybe more than one child. Siblings for Grace. Bella wanted it, the whole family, commitment, forever, fear and all. Luc had protected her the night they made love, but maybe one day...

A low sound of hunger came from Luc's throat. 'I want to get you alone. Maybe not to start on those siblings just yet, but I want you in my arms, nothing held back, no barriers, just the two of us. I want to fall asleep loving you, and wake with you and love you again and know...it isn't going to end.'

He stopped to draw a deep breath. 'I'm sorry I believed the worst of you over your agreement with Maria. You're generous and giving and I couldn't have misjudged you more.'

'Thank you for that. We've both been wrong, but that's behind us now.' In one accord, they moved toward Grace. Bella smiled as Luc's daughter became very still, waiting for them. Then Bella's heart stilled, too, and she reached out her hand to the little girl. 'Would you mind if I started being your new *mamma* right away? I'm not sure I can wait until I've married your father.'

Grace took all of a second to consider the question. 'Yay! Let's go to the house and tell Nanny Heather I've got a new *mamma.*' Then she paused. 'Does this mean I'll get sisters and brothers? I'd like that.'

Luc's arm tightened around Bella's shoulders. 'It's a possibility.'

'Good.' Grace took one of their hands in each of hers and started purposefully back the way she and Luc had come. 'We'll need a party. There can't be a ring and kisses without a party.'

Faces wreathed in smiles, Luc and Bella agreed!

'THIS garden is kind of overpowering, don't you think?' Luc stared around the walled garden at the profusion of flowers, pink being the predominant colour.

The entire garden behind Joe's mechanic shop overflowed with sweet-smelling blooms. 'I've never seen such a bower of manicured plants, shrubs and trees. I'll reek of floral scent for a week after this, I'm certain of it.'

He kept his voice low, so he didn't offend their host.

Joe the mechanic, the host in question, hovered over a charcoal barbecue as he created, according to him, 'masterpieces of culinary delight for our wonderful *alfresco* event together'.

Bella and her sisters seemed to agree about the gastronomic delights. They hadn't left the brawny man's side since he started to cook. Luc could have been jealous of Joe's relationship with his fiancée, soon-to-be-wife. If Bella hadn't explained they were just friends. And if he hadn't discovered her trying to set Joe up with an interesting male she thought he might like.

At Luc's side, Nate Barrett grinned. 'The girls encouraged him to create the garden. Joe gave them his friendship when they first moved here, and that meant a lot to all of them.'

'He has my thanks, too, then.' Luc's attention locked on Bella as she ate a piece of succulent chicken from a kebab stick. His heart raced when she cast him a flirty smile across the group of bodies that separated them.

At his side, Grace tugged on his sleeve to get his attention. He bent down. 'What is it, *piccola?'*

'Can we try the food?' Grace gave him a worry-free gap-toothed grin, easy, happy, childish just as it should be. 'It smells really yummy.'

Luc hoisted his daughter into his arms. 'We can try whatever you like. Maybe your grandmother will have a suggestion as to what we should have first.'

Maria stood beside Bella, and Bella's sisters. The tension that had lurked in his mother's eyes was gone. When she saw their approach, she smiled.

'Here's my little granddaughter.' Pride and pleasure filled her words. Her gaze moved to Luc, and pride and pleasure shone there for him, too.

Grace had accepted the change from aunt to grandmother without concern. Indeed, it had pleased her to have a granny.

'I have lots of relatives, and I'll get more.' Grace made the announcement as Joe retrieved several kebab sticks from the grill, added portions of something mysterious that had been baked in foil, and presented the plates to each of them.

Nate ruffled the little girl's hair. 'That's right. You have a father and a new mother, Grandmother Maria, Aunt Chrissy and Aunt Sophia, and me as your uncle.'

Joe cleared his throat, and Nate went on with barely a pause. 'And an honorary uncle, because Joe is like a brother to Chrissy and Sophia and Bella.'

'Nice save.' Bella cast a teasing grin towards Nate.

Bella was so happy, Luc smiled, too. His fiancée relaxed into life more each day. Her gowns were selling like crazy, she had a staff of four to help with the sewing now, and she needed them!

In his turn, Luc tried to share the decisions with her, big or small, his or hers, because they were a team now. They were both working at co-owning control of things, and getting better at it! He still wanted his wedding band on her finger, and fast, but how could he help that? He simply wanted Bella, in every way there was.

'How's the food?' Joe cast an expectant glance from one face to the next. 'I want to know if the money I invested in the gourmet food course at the local community college was worth it.'

The sisters consumed the final morsels from their plates, kissed their fingers, kissed Joe's clean-shaven cheeks.

'Everything is wonderful.'

'Utterly divine.'

'I've never enjoyed such gastronomic deliciousness.' Sophia uttered this last comment, and her eyes lit with zealous intent. 'I might take a special culinary course, myself. There was a package deal on the internet. You just send your payment and they mail you a DVD of how to cook the food.

'Their aim was to combine as many usually incompatible foods together as possible to make "exotic tastes to provoke every sensation." Doesn't it sound great?'

Chrissy groaned.

Nate asked the details of the website, and said in an aside to his wife, 'Maybe we can get some official food-control people to shut the site down before Soph signs on. There's got to be some law against encouraging the creation of hazardous goods.'

'I heard that.' Soph swished her bright blue hair about her face and tipped her pert nose up until it pointed skyward. 'I'll have you know I'm a very imaginative person in the kitchen.'

This made her sisters and brother-in-law break into chortling guffaws.

When things settled down, Joe raised his can of beer and cleared his throat. 'A toast, as there's another development worth noting in the lives of the sisters Gable.'

Nate made a growling sound in his throat. 'Chrissy's a Barrett now.'

'Yes. I'm referring to their *sisterhood*,' Joe pointed out with painful tolerance. 'The toast isn't about Chrissy, actually, if you'd wait and listen.'

'OK. Go ahead.' Nate draped his arm around his wife's shoulders and smiled into her eyes.

She grinned back—and pinched him on the bottom where Grace's young eyes couldn't see.

Joe cleared his throat again, and moved his gaze to Luc and Bella. Luc reached for his fiancée, drew her against his side and counted his blessings. Bella had moved into the house a week after she accepted his ring. They would be married within the month.

A fast wedding, but Luc refused to wait any longer, and Bella had another team of specialist sewers to assist her with her wedding gown.

Luc's eyes glazed over at the thought of Bella walking down the aisle to him, and his heart swelled with happiness.

'To Arabella and Luchino.' Joe raised his beer can, and the others raised various cans of fizzy drink or beer, depending on the bearer. 'May your marriage be blessed, and if you're looking for a caterer for the event, I might consider helping you out.'

They all laughed, and the sun shone down on their heads, and Luc looked into Bella's eyes and wanted to take her home and to his bed, and keep her there until he ran out of ways to show her how much he loved her.

But that would take forever and beyond.

At Nate's side, Chrissy suddenly stiffened and made an odd sound. One of her hands wrapped around her husband's arm and squeezed, and she forced a lopsided smile. 'Uh, you know how we just discussed how many new relatives Grace has? There's about to be one more. My waters just broke.'

'I'll call an ambulance.' Bella strode to snatch her bag from a chair, fumbled with it and dropped it. 'Ease her into a chair, Nathanial,' she snapped. 'Can't you see the woman is having a baby?'

'My God. Quick. I'll bring the car to the gate.' Nate grasped Chrissy's arms, and then let go to search his pockets frantically for his keys.

Maria rushed to Chrissy's side and began to babble comfort and exhortations—in Italian. Which Chrissy couldn't understand. Bella was trying to learn the language, though, slowly.

Luc snatched Grace up into his arms, grabbed Bella with his free hand, and barked for nobody's benefit in particular, 'Hurry! The baby could happen any second.'

'I'll put the barbecue out.' Joe turned the hose on the barbecue and drowned it, meat, foil-baked delights and all. 'We can go in my four-wheel-drive. It will seat everyone and I can go fast, jump the kerbs if necessary.'

For a crazy moment everyone seemed to run around in circles while Chrissy stood, wide-eyed, a look of wonder and anticipation on her face.

Then Sophia spoke. 'Get a grip on yourselves, all of you!'

The shock of the youngest Gable sister taking charge so thoroughly made them all fall silent and still.

Soph fisted one hand on her hip, and used the other to point a finger at people. 'Joe, get Chrissy some clean towels from your flat. Do it now!'

Joe rushed off to do her bidding.

Her gaze shifted. 'Luc and Bella, you take Grace and Maria

in your car and meet us at the hospital.' She named the hospital Chrissy had chosen for the delivery, and her gaze moved again.

'Nate, your keys are right there in your shirt pocket. Get them, put your wife in the car and drive carefully and sensibly to the hospital. I'll go with Joe and we'll all meet you there.'

At that moment, Chrissy moaned and clutched her abdomen.

Soph drew a sharp breath. 'OK. Make that drive carefully, but as fast as you can manage.'

As they gathered their little family group together to make the trip to the hospital, Bella looked into Luc's eyes. 'I'm about to become an aunty.' A protective glint came into her eye. 'The hospital staff had better take care of my sister.'

'She'll be fine.' Luc planted a quick kiss on her mouth. 'We'll all be there to make sure she is.'

Bella drew a breath and blew it out again. 'OK. You're right. I don't have to panic. I'll only take charge if Nate falls apart or the doctors aren't doing their jobs or...' She trailed off as she hurried towards their waiting car.

And Luchino followed behind her, grinning all the way. 'That's my Arabella.'

HARLEQUIN®

Mediterranean N I G H T S™

Sail aboard the luxurious Alexandra's Dream and experience glamour, romance, mystery and revenge!

Coming in October 2007...

AN AFFAIR TO REMEMBER

by

Karen Kendall

When Captain Nikolas Pappas first fell in love with Helena Stamos, he was a penniless deckhand and she was the daughter of a shipping magnate. But he's never forgiven himself for the way he left her—and fifteen years later, he's determined to win her back.

Though the attraction is still there, Helena is hesitant to get involved. Nick left her once...what's to stop him from doing it again?

www.eHarlequin.com

HM38964

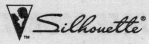

Silhouette®

Romantic

SUSPENSE

Sparked by Danger,
Fueled by Passion.

When evidence is found that Mallory Dawes
intends to sell the personal financial information
of government employees to "the Russian,"
OMEGA engages undercover agent Cutter Smith.
Tailing her all the way to France, Cutter is
fighting a growing attraction to Mallory while at
the same time having to determine her connection
to "the Russian." Is Mallory really the mouse in
this game of cat and mouse?

Look for

Stranded with a Spy

by *USA TODAY* bestselling author

Merline Lovelace

October 2007.

Also available October wherever you buy books:

BULLETPROOF MARRIAGE *(Mission: Impassioned)*
by Karen Whiddon
A HERO'S REDEMPTION *(Haven)* by Suzanne McMinn
TOUCHED BY FIRE by Elizabeth Sinclair

Visit Silhouette Books at www.eHarlequin.com   SRS27553

REQUEST YOUR FREE BOOKS!
2 FREE NOVELS PLUS 2
FREE GIFTS!

HARLEQUIN ROMANCE®

From the Heart, For the Heart

YES! Please send me 2 FREE Harlequin Romance® novels and my 2 FREE gifts. After receiving them, if I don't wish to receive any more books, I can return the shipping statement marked "cancel." If I don't cancel, I will receive 4 brand-new novels every month and be billed just $3.57 per book in the U.S., or $4.05 per book in Canada, plus 25¢ shipping and handling per book and applicable taxes, if any*. That's a savings of over 15% off the cover price! I understand that accepting the 2 free books and gifts places me under no obligation to buy anything. I can always return a shipment and cancel at any time. Even if I never buy another book from Harlequin, the two free books and gifts are mine to keep forever.

114 HDN EEV7   314 HDN EEWK

Name	(PLEASE PRINT)	
Address		Apt.
City	State/Prov.	Zip/Postal Code

Signature (if under 18, a parent or guardian must sign)

Mail to the **Harlequin Reader Service®**:
IN U.S.A.: P.O. Box 1867, Buffalo, NY 14240-1867
IN CANADA: P.O. Box 609, Fort Erie, Ontario L2A 5X3

Not valid to current Harlequin Romance subscribers.

Want to try two free books from another line?
Call 1-800-873-8635 or visit www.morefreebooks.com.

* Terms and prices subject to change without notice. NY residents add applicable sales tax. Canadian residents will be charged applicable provincial taxes and GST. This offer is limited to one order per household. All orders subject to approval. Credit or debit balances in a customer's account(s) may be offset by any other outstanding balance owed by or to the customer. Please allow 4 to 6 weeks for delivery.

Your Privacy: Harlequin is committed to protecting your privacy. Our Privacy Policy is available online at www.eHarlequin.com or upon request from the Reader Service. From time to time we make our lists of customers available to reputable firms who may have a product or service of interest to you. If you would prefer we not share your name and address, please check here. ☐

HR07

Welcome to our newest miniseries, about five
poker players and the women who love them!

Texas Hold'em

When it comes to love, the stakes are high

Beginning October 2007 with

THE BABY GAMBLE

by USA TODAY *bestselling author*

Tara Taylor Quinn

#1446

Desperate to have a baby, Annie Kincaid
turns to the only man she trusts, her ex-husband,
Blake Smith, and asks him to father her child.

Also watch for:

BETTING ON SANTA *by Debra Salonen* November 2007
GOING FOR BROKE *by Linda Style* December 2007
DEAL ME IN *by Cynthia Thomason* January 2008
TEXAS BLUFF *by Linda Warren* February 2008

Look for THE BABY GAMBLE *by* USA TODAY
bestselling author Tara Taylor Quinn.

Available October 2007 wherever you buy books.

www.eHarlequin.com   HSR71446

n o c t u r n e™

Look for
NIGHT MISCHIEF
by
NINA BRUHNS

Lady Dawn Maybank's worst nightmare
is realized when she accidentally conjures
a demon of vengeance, Galen McManus. What
she doesn't realize is that Galen plans to teach
her a lesson in love—one she'll never forget....

DARK
ENCHANTMENTS

Available October wherever you buy books.

Don't miss the last installment of Dark Enchantments,
SAVING DESTINY by Pat White, available November.

www.eHarlequin.com   SN61772

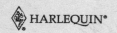

EVERLASTING LOVE™

Every great love has a story to tell™

*An uplifting story of love and survival
that spans generations.*

Hayden MacNulty and Brian Conway
both lived on Briar Hill Road their whole
lives. As children they were destined to
meet, but as a couple Hayden and Brian
have much to overcome before romance
ultimately flourishes.

Look for

*The House on
Briar Hill Road*

by award-winning author

Holly Jacobs

Available October wherever you buy books.

www.eHarlequin.com

HEL65419

Coming Next Month

**Join us in elegant France, stylish Italy
and the rugged Australian mountains! Whether she's having the
boss's baby or being rescued by a millionaire, let Harlequin Romance®
take you from laughter to tears and back again!**

#3979 THE DUKE'S BABY Rebecca Winters
Join gorgeous but scarred Lance, Duc du Lac, in his majestic French
château. He wants nothing more than to hold a child in his arms and be
called "Daddy." Then he meets Andrea, who is pregnant, widowed and
alone....

#3980 THE MEDITERRANEAN REBEL'S BRIDE Lucy Gordon
The Rinucci Brothers
Join Polly on her trip to beautiful Italy as she gives Italian playboy Ruggiero
the news that he's become a father. Can she tame this wild Italian's heart?
Another one of the Rinucci brothers is about to meet his match!

#3981 HER PREGNANCY SURPRISE Susan Meier
Baby on Board
Hardworking Grace never expected to be pregnant with her brooding boss's
child. But in this beautiful story, find out how an unexpected little miracle can
help two people become a loving family of three.

#3982 FOUND: HER LONG-LOST HUSBAND Jackie Braun
Secrets We Keep
It's always hard to admit to your mistakes. Claire has never forgotten her
short-lived marriage to gorgeous Ethan. She sets out to find him and maybe,
just maybe, change their lives forever. Don't miss the last book of the
magnificent Secrets We Keep trilogy.

#3983 THEIR CHRISTMAS WISH COME TRUE Cara Colter
If you love Christmastime and just can't wait for the season to begin, then
don't miss the beautifully heartwarming story of Michael, a man facing his
first Christmas alone. When he volunteers to wrap children's gifts, he meets
Kirsten under the mistletoe....

#3984 MILLIONAIRE TO THE RESCUE Ally Blake
Heart to Heart
If you've ever wanted to be rescued by a knight in shining armor, then this
story is for you. Daniel sweeps brokenhearted and penniless Brooke away to
his luxurious mountain estate. This is one happily ever after you won't want
to miss.

HRCNM0907